Kate hated *not being able to take care of herself.*

And Rick couldn't blame her. If he were honest with himself, he had to admit he would hate it, too.

In fact, if he were honest with himself, he had to admit a lot of things. First, even before she awoke from her coma, he'd admired Kate for raising such a fine son. When she did regain consciousness, he liked her grit and determination. And now…

Now the memory of how sexy Kate looked in her nightgown made Rick fight down a very obvious physiological reaction.

But there was no getting away from it: He was attracted to her.

Kate was still hurting, still battered, still bruised. And if he wanted her—along with her little boy—now, what was going to happen when Kate was well and whole and even more desirable?

Dear Reader,

We've been trying to capture what Silhouette Romance means to our readers, our authors and ourselves. In canvassing some authors, I've heard wonderful words about the characteristics of a Silhouette Romance novel—innate tenderness, lively, thoughtful, fun, emotional, hopeful, satisfying, warm, sparkling, genuine and affirming.

It pleases me immensely that our writers are proud of their line and their readers! And I hope you're equally delighted with their offerings. Be sure to drop a line or visit our Web site and let us know what we're doing right—and any particular favorite topics you want to revisit.

This month we have another fantastic lineup filled with variety and strong writing. We have a new continuity—HAVING THE BOSS'S BABY! Judy Christenberry's *When the Lights Went Out...* starts off the series about a powerful executive's discovery that one woman in his office is pregnant with his child. But who could it be? Next month Elizabeth Harbison continues the series with *A Pregnant Proposal.*

Other stories for this month include Stella Bagwell's conclusion to our MAITLAND MATERNITY spin-off. Go find *The Missing Maitland.* Raye Morgan's popular office novels continue with *Working Overtime.* And popular Intimate Moments author Beverly Bird delights us with an amusing tale about *Ten Ways To Win Her Man.*

Two more emotional titles round out the month. With her writing partner, Debrah Morris wrote nearly fifteen titles for Silhouette Books as Pepper Adams. Now she's on her own with *A Girl, a Guy and a Lullaby.* And Martha Shields's dramatic stories always move me. Her *Born To Be a Dad* opens with an unusual, powerful twist and continues to a highly satisfying ending!

Enjoy these stories, and keep in touch.

Mary-Theresa Hussey

Mary-Theresa Hussey,
Senior Editor

Please address questions and book requests to:
Silhouette Reader Service
U.S.: 3010 Walden Ave., P.O. Box 1325, Buffalo, NY 14269
Canadian: P.O. Box 609, Fort Erie, Ont. L2A 5X3

Born To Be a Dad

MARTHA SHIELDS

SILHOUETTE *Romance*®

Published by Silhouette Books

America's Publisher of Contemporary Romance

To my cousin, Diane Shuttlesworth, RN, ESN, Trauma/ICU nurse at Memorial Regional Hospital in Hollywood, Florida, and avid romance reader. Thanks for all your help!

 SILHOUETTE BOOKS

ISBN 0-373-19551-6

BORN TO BE A DAD

Visit Silhouette at www.eHarlequin.com

Printed in U.S.A.

Books by Martha Shields

Silhouette Romance

*Home Is Where Hank Is #1287
*And Cowboy Makes Three #1317
*The Million-Dollar Cowboy #1346
Husband Found #1377
The Princess and the Cowboy #1403
Lassoed! #1461
The Blacksheep Prince's Bride #1510
Born To Be a Dad #1551

*Cowboys to the Rescue

MARTHA SHIELDS

grew up telling stories to her sister to pass the time on long drives to their grandparents' house. Since she's never been able to stop dreaming up characters, she's thrilled to share her stories with a wider audience. Martha lives in Memphis, Tennessee. She has a master's degree in journalism and works at a local university, where her job includes graphic design.

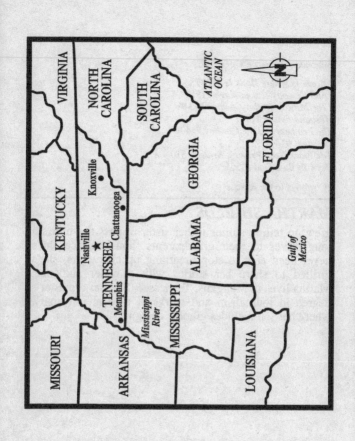

Chapter One

Rick McNeal slammed on his brakes and jerked his steering wheel to the left to avoid the boy on the bike, riding on the wrong side of the road and heading straight at him. The boy veered toward the sidewalk and whished past Rick's Jeep as it screeched to a stop.

Rick squeezed his eyes in relief. He'd missed him. Thank God.

He opened his eyes to find his hands clutching the wheel, trembling with the fatigue that had finally driven him home from Data Enterprises. He peeled them off and took a deep breath.

Then he replaced his hands. He had to move. This wasn't the busiest street in Memphis this late, but—

Suddenly the world whirled around him as a car clipped the back corner of his Jeep, sending him spinning into the oncoming lane. Rick caught a glimpse of a young woman's horrified face as his Jeep spun around and slammed into her door.

Another set of tires squealed before a huge black Cadillac smashed into the compact's rear end, then tailed into him.

The Jeep whirled. His front end struck the compact again. Airbags burst from his dashboard, forcing him to release control of the steering wheel.

When the twirling finally stopped, he sat, stunned.

His first lucid thought was a brief prayer that he hadn't turned over, hadn't been hurt.

His second was for the boy on the bike. Had he escaped all of that?

After he took a few seconds to get his bearings, a glance in the rearview mirror showed the boy hightailing it down the hill as fast as his legs could pedal, throwing horrified glances over his shoulder.

Rick's third realization came as he pulled his eyes from the rearview mirror and scanned the immediate area. The Cadillac's driver was already climbing out of his vehicle, surveying his crumpled hood and skewed rear bumper. But the first car that hit him—an older, foreign compact—hadn't been nearly as lucky as either one of them.

Through the haze of dust from the now-collapsed airbag, he saw the small car lying on its side, the roof severely dented by the curb it rested against. One headlight was out. The other hung by a wire, lighting up a tumbling mass of shimmering blond hair through the windshield.

The scene was horribly, sickeningly familiar.

The memory of another accident—three years earlier—flashed across Rick's mind. That accident had fatally injured his wife and unborn son.

"No!"

Dear God, this couldn't be happening again.

He struggled to open his door but was hampered by the dented frame. Turning to add the power of his legs, he realized he was still caught in the restraint of the seat belt that had saved his life—the life that for three years hadn't been worth drawing breath.

He released the latch and finally forced the Jeep's door

open. Scrambling down, he lurched across pavement littered with glass and unidentifiable car parts to the small hunk of twisted metal barely recognizable as an automobile.

Halfway there, he heard the sounds of soft rock music drifting from the shattered windows. The radio was probably the only part of the car that still worked. Then he heard something far more ominous. A child's voice softly crying for its mother.

Arriving at the car, he didn't know what to do. Should he try to pull them from the wreckage? Or would he cause more injury?

"I've called 9-1-1. Are you all right?"

Rick turned to see the Cadillac's driver standing beside him. Dazed, he looked around. People were making their way out of homes in this upper-middle-class neighborhood in east Memphis.

"I'm fine," he insisted impatiently. "I just don't know if we should—"

"Look out!"

The woman's cry warned them seconds before a sports car came flying over the hill. The young man driving slammed on his brakes and swerved. He avoided rear-ending the Cadillac, but crashed into the compact.

The impact shoved the small car forward another ten yards. The screech of metal on pavement felt like razors slicing into Rick's skin.

The compact wobbled precariously, then landed on all four wheels which, miraculously, were still inflated. It bounced several times, then went still.

Rick fought free of the man who'd pulled him away from the newest collision. He ran to the compact with the Cadillac driver close behind.

"We've got to get them out," Rick said.

"What if they're injured?" the man asked.

Rick pointed to the sports car. "What if that happens again? They could be killed."

He didn't finish his thought out loud, *if they aren't already*.

The Cadillac driver took a step back. "I've heard of people who helped and then got sued because they did something wrong."

"Then don't help." Rick didn't care if they sued him. It wasn't as if he didn't deserve it. Nothing he had was worth anything to him anymore, anyway. He'd gladly give it all to them if he could just save their lives.

The man pulled at his sleeve. "You can't—"

"Hey, man!" The young driver emerged from his sports car. He was bleeding from a cut above his eye. "I didn't see it until I was right on it."

Rick waved in the young man's direction. "Go help him."

The Cadillac driver hurried away, leaving Rick free to do what he could.

The crying from inside was louder now.

Rick peered in the back window to the only unscathed part of the car, where a frightened little boy was still strapped in a sturdy car seat in the middle of the back seat.

Thank God for a caring mother.

The car seat was surrounded with plastic bags. A rip in one told Rick the boy had been cushioned by clothes.

When Rick opened the door, the little boy stopped crying and thrust his arms toward him. His dark blue eyes were wide with fright and his face was streaked with tears. "Out! Out! Out!"

Rick's heart tumbled over as he tossed bags of clothes onto the asphalt so he could free the boy. "Hush, little guy. You're all right. Everything's going to be fine."

As soon as he was freed, the boy scrambled into Rick's arms and held on tight, like a baby monkey to its mother.

Rick squeezed back and whispered a thankful prayer the boy wasn't injured.

"Mommy!" the boy cried. "Get my mommy out, too!"

"What's your name, son?" Rick asked.

"Jo—" He sniffed a sobbing breath. "Jo—" His voice broke on a sob again. "Joey."

"You're a brave boy, Joey. I'm proud of you." He threw a pleading glance at a woman standing on the curb.

Understanding, she hurried over to help.

"Joey, will you be brave one more time and let this lady hold you?"

Joey clung tighter. "Help my mommy."

"I can't help your mommy unless you go with this lady. She's not going to take you far. Okay?"

Joey sniffed on a broken sob again. "'Kay."

He clung for another second, then loosed his hold enough for Rick to hand him over.

"Can you get someone to bring blankets?" Rick nodded meaningfully toward the crowd at the curb. He didn't want Joey to see his mother's condition…whatever it was.

The middle-aged woman nodded, then cooed to the boy as Rick bent to peer at Joey's mother.

On the other side of a window splintered around the clear indent of her head, a slender young woman lay slumped against her seat belt. Her long, silvery blond hair was streaked with blood, but the otherwise shimmering strands covered too much of her for Rick to determine further injuries.

She was unconscious at best. At worst—

He halted the thought, refusing to go there.

She had to be alive…for Joey's sake.

And for his own.

He couldn't bear being responsible for the death of another young woman. The small part of him that was still alive would shrivel and die.

The need for urgency dragged Rick's mind back to the present. Glancing down, he saw that the door handle had been sheared off. The back door was still hanging open, so he went around and tried to reach forward to release the inside door handle, but his arm was a couple of inches too short.

He had just rejected the idea of releasing the young woman's seat belt so she could slump to the side and give him room when she moaned.

Rick froze. "Hello? Can you hear me? Are you all right?"

"I…" She moaned again.

Thank God she was alive.

Spying a worn baby blanket in Joey's car seat, Rick grabbed it, wrapped it around his hand, then bashed the driver's window open from the inside. He stepped back outside the car and shut the back door just as another car slammed on its brakes as it came over the hill. This one narrowly missed the wreckage.

Rick yelled at the men standing on the sidewalk. "Rig up some kind of warning system for oncoming cars, will you?"

One of them nodded, then dragged several others away.

Rick turned his attention back to Joey's mother. Her right hand was faintly, futilely tugging at the seat belt across her chest.

"Don't." Rick reached inside the broken window and unlatched her door. "I'll get you out."

She let her hand fall to her lap. "Pl-please."

"Don't worry, ma'am. I'm going to help you."

He leaned in and gently lifted her head. When he pushed the hair from her face, he winced at the gash starting at her left temple and extending into her hair.

Her right eye opened and regarded him with an intensely blue gaze. "Joe…my son. Please."

Rick's heart nearly broke. As injured as she was, her first thought was for her child. Her selflessness, as well as the sound of another set of screeching brakes, renewed his determination to save her. "Joey's fine. He's already out of the car."

Her one good eye closed in relief.

"We're in a dangerous position here. I need to get you out. Is that all right? Are you too injured? Hello?"

She must've lost consciousness again, for there was no reply.

Rick hesitated. Was she too badly injured to move? Was he making an even bigger mistake by trying?

"Here's a couple of blankets," a man said behind him. "How's she doing in there?"

"She was conscious for a few seconds," Rick replied. "I was just wondering if I should—"

The squeal of more brakes decided him. She was seriously injured. No doubt about that. But she'd be a hell of a lot safer lying on the grass away from the danger zone.

He turned to the man. "I've got to get her out before someone else isn't able to stop."

"Need some help?"

Relieved, Rick reached for the blankets.

The numbing darkness beckoned. Kate longed to sink into its sanctuary…down…down…away from the pain searing through her head and driving up the left side of her body.

But she couldn't.

Joey had no one but her. He was too small, too helpless. She couldn't desert him.

They were strangers in a strange city about to become their home. But even if she knew someone she could count on to take care of him, she wouldn't know how to ask. She never asked for help from anyone, for anything. Not since she'd been old enough to take care of herself.

A cacophony of noises made the darkness seem even more seductive. Sirens screaming. People talking, shouting.

But above it all, a single voice stood out. Or rather, below it all. Because The Voice was very deep, very soothing.

She concentrated on The Voice, so close, until the pain caught her and snapped her into consciousness.

"Hang on, please." The sounds The Voice uttered finally formed into words. "The ambulance is almost here. Joey's all right and he needs—"

She groaned.

"Ma'am? Are you awake again?"

The pain nearly sent her diving again into the darkness.

"What's your name? Can you tell me?"

Something she could wrap her mind around, something to keep her from the dark, inviting depths. "K-Kate."

It seemed she'd shouted the word, but the soothing voice demanded it again. "What?"

She drew a deep, painful breath and repeated, "Kate."

"Kate." The soothing voice held approval. "Kate what?"

She wanted the calm quality of The Voice to continue. She needed The Voice. It held the hint of promises...that Joey would be okay...that she would be okay.

She took another deep breath. The pain didn't surprise her this time. "Burnett."

"Kate Burnett. You're doing fine. Is there anyone I should call?"

Kate thought she shook her head but evidently didn't because The Voice repeated, "Kate? Who do I call and tell what happened? I noticed you have a Madison County license plate. Is there someone there who'll be worried?"

She licked her dry lips, then took another breath. "No...no. Just...Joe."

"What about his father?"

"No...father. Gone."

She heard a low curse, then The Voice said, "Hang on, Kate. The ambulance just pulled up."

"No." She tried to lift her left arm, but it wouldn't cooperate, so she lifted the right and rested her hand on a thick, well-muscled leg.

She hated what she was about to do. She'd sworn since she was eighteen that she would never ask anyone for anything ever again. But her pride didn't matter now. She had to keep Joey out of the hands of the state.

Because her mother had been so often out of a job, Kate had intimate knowledge of how states handled children—

with indifference at best, but often with worse neglect than they accused the parents of showing. She'd promised her son on the day he was born that she'd always be there to take care of him.

"Joey."

A large hand swallowed hers. "Joey's all right. He's not injured."

"Joey," she repeated. With tremendous effort, she opened her eyes, though only the right one focused. The man who knelt beside her was darkly handsome. His square jaw was tight, and deep worry lines surrounded his thickly lashed brown eyes.

How could she ask him? How could she ask anyone?

He glanced up, then back down. "The ambulance is here. They'll take care of you."

She *had* to ask. Now. "Don't let them…anyone…take him…Joey…please."

He squeezed her hand. "Don't worry, Kate. I'll take care of Joey myself. For as long as you need me to. It's the least I can do after—"

"Sir, if you'll move away so we can get to her…"

The man with The Voice nodded at someone above them, then glanced back down at her. "I'll bring Joey to the hospital as soon as I've dealt with the police. Don't worry at all about him. He's safe with me."

"I…please…" She tried to keep his hand in hers, but she was too weak.

Then The Voice was gone.

The EMTs began their probing assessment of her injuries, causing pain to scream inside her head. The darkness wrapped its numbing arms around her and gently pulled her into the murky depths.

Guilt followed her down. She was leaving her son in the hands of a stranger.

But what else could she do?

Keep Joey safe!

She sent the silent plea to the man she only knew as The

Voice and, somehow, she was sure he would take good care of her son.

Rick stood at the plate-glass window, staring unblinkingly into room seven of the intensive care unit of Baptist Hospital.

Kate Burnett lay between pristine white sheets. Wires of every color and tubes of every size protruded from her, hooked up to machines surrounding her slender, unmoving body.

Her left arm—fractured in three places, both above and below the elbow—was encased in a splint. Her left leg had been immobilized in traction, with steel rods holding the thigh bone together.

She looked so pale, so fragile with her wavy, blond hair flowing from beneath the white bandage obliterating half of her face. At least, it flowed on the right side of her head. He knew the left side had been partially shaved so the doctors could assess her injuries and put in eighteen stitches to close the gash there. The skull beneath it had been cracked, but the doctors could find no evidence of bone penetrating her brain.

What kind of woman was she? Would she throw a fit when she learned half of her beautiful hair was gone? Or would she count the loss as a blessing, since she'd survived?

His fatigued mind concentrated on the meaningless, unanswerable questions so he wouldn't think about how much the woman lying in the ICU bed reminded him of Stacy, so he wouldn't give in to the urge to flee.

His wife had died in a similar bed three years earlier. Not that the two women looked anything alike. Stacy had had dark hair and coal-black eyes.

But he'd put both of them in that hospital bed.

My fault. My fault. My fault.

The litany had been running through Rick's head ever since he'd climbed from his Jeep.

He'd been on a long visit to hell the past eight hours. Or rather, he'd been driven deeper into the flames. He'd been in hell for three years—ever since he'd watched the nurses disconnect the life support from his wife's body.

My fault.

Everyone—the police, his mother, even Stacy's parents—had assured him the accident hadn't been his fault.

But this one was. He felt the guilt deeper than his bones, though police officers at the scene assured him he wasn't at fault.

Fatigue from too many hours of work had dulled his senses. He'd worked hard to build his software company, worked himself to exhaustion…to a blessed state of oblivion. On purpose.

But the fatigue had a side effect he hadn't counted on. It slowed his reaction time. If he'd seen the kid on the bike a second earlier, or if he'd had enough wits to get the hell out of the road…

But he hadn't.

Rick's attention focused again on Kate and he thought of her son, who lay sleeping in the ICU waiting room, watched over by one of the nurses.

Half of his mind screamed at him to leave both the mother and the boy and run. Run from the hospital that held such terrible memories. Run from the steady bleep of the heart monitor that could stop any second. Run from the smell of antiseptic death.

He couldn't go through this again. He couldn't stand here and watch another woman die.

The irony wasn't lost on him. The very thing that had kept him sane was threatening to drive him to insanity once again.

He'd been working twelve to eighteen hours a day for the past three years, hoping to forget his wife's screams, hoping to forget the lonely silence that filled his days and the nightmares that plagued his nights.

He'd been successful…to a degree. Algorithms and gigabytes had pushed his sorrow away during the day, and exhaustion had blessed him with dreamless nights.

But his success had caused an even bigger failure. The evidence of which was lying there in the hospital bed.

Kate Burnett.

Even through a thick glass and a distance of six feet, he could see the pale translucence of her skin. She looked like a porcelain doll—broken and lifeless.

No! his mind insisted. Not lifeless. Not this time.

Though he'd told the doctors to spare no expense, that he'd pay all her bills, they could give him no reassurance of her recovery.

Heads wounds, they'd said, were unpredictable injuries. She could wake tomorrow with nothing more than a severe headache, or she could lie in a coma for years.

My fault. My fault. My fault.

Rick felt helpless. The only thing he could do for Kate was take care of her son.

The boy had clung to him ever since Rick reclaimed him from the woman who'd held him while Rick had taken care of Kate. When the police questioned him, they assumed Joey was his son, not Kate's.

Rick let them assume all they wanted. He'd promised Kate he'd take care of her son, and he would fight anyone who tried to take the boy away from him. Luckily, he didn't even have to lie.

While the two of them sat for hours in the ICU waiting room, Joey told Rick about moving to Memphis from Jackson, Tennessee, about the new "school" he'd be attending while his mother worked, about their plans for his fifth birthday in June.

Rick bought Joey crackers and juice from the snack machines, then the boy had fallen asleep, curled against his chest.

Amazing, how kids could sleep through anything.

Now he was glad Joey was asleep so he couldn't insist on seeing his mother. The sight of her lying so still and pale might frighten him. At the very least, Joey would want to go to her, to touch her, to make sure she was okay.

Rick knew, because that's what half of him wanted to do—the half that wasn't trying to talk him into fleeing.

But the nurses had been adamant about his staying out of the room. They'd only allowed him this far because Rick had insisted so long and so loudly.

"I'm sorry," he murmured as he leaned against the glass. "I didn't mean to hurt you."

I know.

The soft feminine voice whispering in his mind startled him. He straightened and gaped at the injured woman. It was Kate's voice. He knew the sound, though he hadn't heard her utter twenty words.

Rick shook his head to rid his exhausted brain of the notion. It was just fatigue again, playing tricks on him.

Take care of Joey. Please.

Alarmed, Rick peered closely at Kate. He could hear her voice so clearly. Was it his imagination, or had her head turned slightly toward him?

He shook his head again, with a sigh of disgust. Communicating telepathically with a comatose woman?

Right. Next he'd believe CPUs fell in love with each other.

A hand on Rick's arm startled him.

"There's nothing you can do here," a nurse said kindly. "Go home and get some rest. Take care of your son. We'll do everything we can for your lady."

The hospital staff had been assuming all night that he and Kate were attached. Rick hadn't corrected them, other than telling them his last name, which was obviously different from hers. "Thank you. I will."

The nurse smiled and walked away.

He turned to the glass once more. "Concentrate on getting well, beautiful Kate. And until you wake, I'll take care of Joey like he *is* my own son."

I know.

Rick peered closely at her again. He wanted to believe she was communicating with him. He wanted to believe she forgave him.

But she was unconscious. She didn't know anything.

He shook his head and returned to the waiting room. When he lifted Joey from the couch, the boy curled a tiny arm around his neck.

Rick peered down at the utterly relaxed face.

Joey's mouth was open slightly, drooling on Rick's shirt.

Rick's heart rose to his throat, and he placed a reassuring hand on Joey's small back.

Poor little guy. His first night in a new town and he was involved in an accident that took his mother away.

Rick patted Joey's back. "Come on, little guy. Both of us need a nice, warm bed and a good night's sleep."

Chapter Two

The wake-up smells of bacon and coffee penetrated Rick's dreams, tantalizing him from sleep.

He smiled. Must be Sunday. Sunday was the only day he didn't work, the only day he could sleep in.

When his mother was in town, she drove over to make him a big Sunday breakfast, then they went to chur—

He bolted upright.

Joey.

The bedside clock told Rick it was after ten.

Was the boy up?

He shoved his hand back through his hair, trying to force his sleep-dulled mind into gear.

Probably. Rick hadn't put the little guy to bed in his town house's guest bedroom until nearly dawn, but Joey had zonked out at the hospital so he'd gotten far more sleep.

No telling what his mother was thinking.

Rick slipped on a fresh pair of khakis and hurried downstairs.

The scene he came upon was so reminiscent of the

dreams he'd had before Stacy died, it stopped him cold in the doorway.

Alice McNeal wore an apron over her deep-red silk Sunday dress. Her salt-and-pepper hair was still perfectly coifed from her Friday-afternoon salon appointment. She stood at the stove with her back to him, explaining to Joey how she knew when it was time to turn pancakes.

Joey sat on the counter beside her, fascinated by the subject far more than any four-year-old boy should be.

Alice looked like an adoring grandmother, exactly the way Rick had pictured she would look as she cooked breakfast for his son—the child who'd died with Stacy.

Stunned by the unexpected resurfacing of a painful memory he'd buried deep, Rick clutched the doorjamb.

The movement made Joey glance up. He brightened instantly. "Rick! Guess what? Miz Alice makes pancakes that look like Mickey Mouse!"

Alice turned. The glasses she wore only when she wanted to do some "serious seeing" couldn't cover the wistfulness in her eyes, though she tried to distract Rick with sarcasm. "Well, if it isn't Rip Van Winkle."

Joey giggled. "Rip Van Winkle slept for a hunnert years and had a long beard when he woke up. Rick doesn't have a beard." The boy's face twisted as he peered closer at Rick, then amended, "Much."

"The kid knows his fairy tales." Alice patted the boy approvingly with the hand not holding the spatula. "Joey knows a lot of things. More than you ever knew at this age."

Rick made his hand release the jamb, then he headed toward the coffee pot. "Why didn't you wake me?"

"Because I thought you already were awake when I walked in the door to smell coffee. Imagine my surprise when I walked into the kitchen to find a four-year-old boy had made it instead of a thirty-three-year-old man."

"I'm almost five!" Joey said proudly.

Rick paused at his mother's comment. "*Joey* made the coffee?"

She nodded. "It was ready by the time I arrived. Looked like it had been ready for some time."

Rick turned his amazement on the boy. "You're only four. When did you learn to make coffee?"

Joey scrunched into a whole-body shrug. "I dunno. I make it for Mommy when she's gettin' ready for work."

"You don't drink it, do you?"

He shook his head vigorously and pointed to a glass on the counter with a thin white film coating the sides. "I had me some milk."

"Good." Rick was impressed by the boy's ability to take care of himself. He'd noticed the night before that Joey acted years older than his age. His mother was certainly doing a good job raising him.

His determination to do everything he could to help the woman lying in the hospital renewed, Rick once again headed for the coffee. As he reached for a mug in the cabinet above, his mother placed the last pancake on the piled plate, then turned off the burner and moved the pan off the stove.

"Can I carry them to the table?" Joey asked.

Alice glanced dubiously from his small arms to the laden platter. "Think you can manage all this?"

He nodded. "I carry plates all the time."

"All right, then."

Anticipating her, Rick stepped over and lifted the boy down from the counter.

Alice set the platter on Joey's small arms, then they stood side by side watching the boy slowly carry his precious cargo to the breakfast nook in the bay window.

His mother's voice lowered. "Heavens, Rick. Have you taken a good look at this child? He's the very image of you at his age."

Rick frowned. He hadn't noticed how much the boy

looked like him. He'd been too distracted the night before. But now that she'd mentioned it...

"He could be your son. He could be..." Alice's reverent whisper trailed off. "He's almost the right age. Just a year older than Jeremy would've been."

His mother might as well have hit him in the chest with a sledgehammer.

Joey turned after placing the pancakes on the table and proved there was nothing wrong with his ears. "Who's Jeremy?"

Rick cleared his throat. "A little boy who died before he was born."

"Oh." The boy chewed on Rick's statement as he ambled toward them, but the puzzle was obviously too much for him. "Huh?"

Alice came to Rick's rescue. "You like maple syrup on your pancakes, Joey?"

"Yes, ma'am."

Rick picked up his mug of coffee, then reached into the refrigerator for the half-and-half. It was in the same place he always kept it, so his hand touched the carton instantly.

The small, everyday motions soothed him, brought back the control that had held him together for the past three years.

Jeremy was the name he and Stacy had chosen if their child had been a boy. She'd miscarried two days before she died, and the doctors had thought he would want to know he almost had a son. Some days he wondered if that was the special purgatory designed for him—knowing what might have been.

Not knowing the sex of his child would have been infinitely better. He wouldn't have put a face to the name, wouldn't have played baseball with the shadow of Jeremy in his mind.

Now every memory he would *never* have crystallized...into Joey. It was as if his child had been born to another mother...then found his way home.

Rick shook the ridiculous notion from his head.

Joey was not his child. He belonged to Kate Burnett, who was going to recover soon and take the boy away.

Rick turned back to Alice. "Did Joey tell you why he's here?"

"He said something about an accident. Being turned upside down and sirens and ambulances—"

"And police guys ever'where," Joey added.

Alice's frown deepened. "Sounds serious."

Rick felt his guilt anew and didn't try to hide it from his mother. "It was. It was also my fault."

His mother knew the self-reproach he'd lived with for three years. She shook her head. "No, Rick. It wasn't."

Knowing she was talking about the accident three years ago, he gave her as graphic a recounting of this one as he could with a four-year-old in the room.

Joey added his own comments, mostly about his experiences as the car spun and rolled over—which only made Rick feel worse.

Joey dug the knife deeper when he said in a still, small voice, "When we got still, Mommy wouldn't talk to me."

Tears glistened in Alice's brown eyes as she gathered Joey into one arm and Rick into the other. "Oh, my dear, sweet boys. I can't believe it."

Her unconditionally loving arms felt like a warm quilt on a freezing winter night. "It's true. All of it."

"It wasn't your fault, Rick," she insisted. "You were hit from behind. Besides, that boy on the bike is mostly to blame. Riding in the middle of the street like that. What happened to him?"

"He left as quickly as he could," Rick said. "I saw him in my rearview mirror. No one knew who he was."

She kissed Rick's cheek and then bent to kiss Joey's. "Don't you worry. Everything's going to be all right."

Rick didn't know if his mother was talking to him or Joey, but it didn't matter. They both needed reassuring.

"Mommy's gonna be okay, too." Joey's statement was emphatic. There was absolutely no doubt in his voice.

Rick was impressed with the boy's innate optimism. Kate Burnett really had done an excellent job raising his son.

His mind's Freudian slip gave Rick a jolt.

Her son. This was Joey *Burnett*, not Jeremy McNeal.

Kate swam in a sea of darkness just below the threshold of consciousness, agitated, restless.

Something beckoned her urgently across the threshold, but she couldn't go. Every time she tried, the pain of a thousand ice picks stabbing through her brain drove her back.

She couldn't tell exactly what it was that beckoned, yet she knew it was vitally important.

Every now and then voices would hover over her. She didn't recognize them, so it didn't seem worth the concentration it would take to understand what they were saying, but they seemed concerned.

After they came, there would be a period of silence, of blackness. Then Kate would slowly start drifting toward the threshold again—wanting but not daring to cross. Though every time she surfaced, consciousness seemed more critical.

She had no way of knowing how long this period of anxious restlessness continued, but she did know when it ended. It ended when The Voice returned.

"Kate?"

Her attention—which had been unable to focus—latched on to the deep timbre. She hadn't known until this moment that she'd been waiting to hear this sound.

"I know you probably can't hear me, Kate, but perhaps on some level you can understand what I'm saying."

She felt pressure on her hand. Warmth enveloped it, where before there had been only cold.

"Joey's okay. They won't let me bring a four-year-old into intensive care. You wouldn't want him to see you like this, anyway. But I helped him make a tape. Here. Just a sec... Let me push this...."

"Mommy?" A pause. "Is she there?"

"It's not like the phone," The Voice said. "She won't talk back, but she'll be able to hear what you say."

Suddenly Kate knew why she'd been anxious.

Joey. Her son. Her Joey needed her.

"Hi, Mommy. I'm here with Alice and Rick. You know what? Rick's got a swimming pool! Course it's too cold to go swimmin' now. But he says I can go this summer. You can come, too. It's not just his, though. Alice says it b'longs to the 'partment com-com..."

A feminine voice coached him.

"...plex. Anyways, other kids go swimmin' there, too. Cool, huh?"

The feminine voice said something else.

"Oh, yeah. Alice says to tell you I'm fine. She's gonna take care of me. She makes pancakes in the shape of Mickey Mouse! I helped her, then I ate 'em up. And Rick's gonna bring me to the hospital when you wake up."

"Anything else you want to say?" The Voice asked.

"I love you, Mommy. Wake up soon, 'kay?"

A click ended the blessed sound, then The Voice spoke again, closer. "We're taking good care of him, Kate, so don't worry. My mother, Alice McNeal, is a grandmother waiting to happen. She's thrilled to have a youngster to take care of. She's going to keep him during the day while I'm at work. Says it's practice for when she has her own. Of course, I don't know when that will happen, since I'm her only child, and I'm..."

He let the sentence drift off. "Like you care about any of that. Like you can even hear what I'm saying. I just...I just thought it might help you get well if you knew Joey is in good hands. And he is. The best. She raised me, after all."

"Yeah, right. Like I'm a prize." He chuckled nervously. "But my mother is. She's the best."

He sighed. "Okay. I guess I'd better get going. They just gave me a minute to come in and see how you're doing. I'll be back later today. They'll let me stay longer then. I'll insist."

The warmth and pressure on her hand increased for a second.

"You *have* to get well, Kate. Joey needs you." The Voice cracked slightly. "I need you to get well, too. You don't know how much."

Then The Voice was gone…and so was Kate's restlessness.

Now she knew she didn't have to cross the threshold, didn't have to face the ice picks until she was strong enough. The Voice was keeping Joey safe, and that's all that mattered.

When he entered ICU that night, Rick stopped by the nurses' station.

"Good evening, Mr. McNeal," the pretty strawberry blonde said.

"Hi, Diane." He nodded toward Kate's room in the southeast corner. All of the rooms could be seen from the nurse's station. "Any change?"

She glanced at him, then toward Kate's room. "Well…"

"She woke?" he asked quickly.

"No, no. Nothing like that. It's just that she's been resting better since your visit this afternoon."

"Since my visit? Really?" When Diane nodded, he asked, "Does that mean she's going to be okay?"

The nurse hesitated. "I can't tell you anything more than the doctor on duty last night told you. Head wounds are unpredictable. Her resting better could mean she's slipped deeper into a coma, or it could mean that something was bothering her subconsciously and now it's not and she's decided not to fight the healing she needs to do. We'll just have to wait and see."

"Wait and see," Rick murmured. "That seems to be the favorite phrase around here."

"I'm sorry. It's just that I—"

"That's okay, Diane. I know you can't offer false hope." He looked at the clock on the wall behind her. "I can stay longer tonight, then, right? The whole visiting hour?"

She smiled. "Unless she becomes restless again."

"Okay. Thanks."

Rick's steps were silent on the industrial-grade carpet as he made his way to Kate's room. Nothing more than a glass cubicle, really, so the nurses could keep a close eye on their patients.

He stood inside the door. Nothing had changed since his visit in the early afternoon.

Kate Burnett still lay unmoving beneath taut sheets. The half of her face he could see seemed as if it had been carved from the purest white marble. If a single blond hair had shifted, he couldn't tell. The changes the nurses had noticed must've been visible only to the machines monitoring every breath, every heartbeat.

He drew alongside the rail of her bed and reached down to cover her hand with his, careful not to disturb the clip attached to her finger. "You're going to be fine, aren't you, Kate? You haven't slipped further away from us. Joey's voice reassured you, didn't it?"

He waited—half expecting the low, cool voice that had echoed through his brain the night before. But there was only silence.

He frowned. He'd known it was all in his head. Still...

He shook his head and sighed. "It's been a long— Geez. It hasn't even been twenty-four hours, yet, has it?"

Rick studied the classic lines of her face, mottled with bruises. "Who are you, Kate Burnett? I've heard that nothing happens that isn't meant to happen, and every little choice we make has a reason. If that's true, why did I do this to you? What possible good can come from you lying in this hospital?"

With his forefinger, he traced the straight line of her nose, the indentation of her cheek between the bone her pale eyelashes rested on and the sharply defined curve of her jaw. "You're so young and so beautiful. And such a wonderful mother. I can tell by your son. He's incredibly intelligent. My mother said she's never seen a little boy talk like Joey. He seems more like he's seven or eight than four. Excuse me. Almost five. What did you do? Read him the encyclopedia when he was still in a crib? He's a good boy, too. Full of laughter and hope and questions."

Unconsciously leaning closer, Rick stared at the mother of the boy he'd taken in. "I should be the one lying there, not you. You have everything to live for and I—"

He broke off, having promised himself years ago that he wouldn't go there. He had his mother, as she often reminded him, and his health and his software company.

But no family. No wife. No son.

"Is that why you came into my life?" he asked Kate. "To remind me? I was buried so deep in my job I'd almost forgotten to grieve every hour of every day. But I crash into you, and it all comes flooding back."

He dropped his head and forced the memories away.

"Sorry," he said after a long moment. "You certainly didn't ask to crash into my life, did you? The accident was my fault. I have no doubt about that, even if everyone else says it isn't."

He trailed off and raised his gaze back to her face. "I feel like an idiot. Like I'm talking to myself."

He watched her take several shallow breaths. "I don't know if I should keep coming to see you or not. I've heard about injured people who aren't expected to recover, and a loved one comes in every day and talks to them like they were awake, and then one day they wake up and remember everything that was said."

He rubbed a hand across his jaw. "But I guess the key phrase is *loved one*. You don't even know who I am.

Funny, though, I feel as if I know you. At least, as if I'm beginning to. I guess because of all Joey's told me.''

Rick took her hand gently. "For what it's worth, Kate—if you can hear me—Joey's doing fine. I'll bring him to see you as soon as they'll let me."

"I almost forgot. Joey told me to give you a kiss from him, so here it is." He leaned over and kissed her cool cheek.

That launched him into a monologue about Joey, how he and Alice had taken the boy to the park then to McDonalds for an early supper before Alice took him to the night service at church while Rick came back to the hospital. He talked until Diane came in and told him it was past time to leave.

Surprised by how fast the time had flown, Rick gazed down at the pale, utterly still woman on the bed. "Guess I have to go."

He sighed. "I don't know if I'm helping or hurting by coming, so until I know, I guess I'll keep coming. See you tomorrow, Kate Burnett."

Tomorrow.

Rick frowned at the form lying so still on the bed. Either he was going crazy or this was the most remarkable woman he'd ever run into.

He smiled wryly at his choice of words.

Perhaps it was a little of both.

He walked slowly to the door, then stopped and glanced over his shoulder. Odd. He was reluctant to leave.

He wanted to stay and talk to Kate about buying Joey clothes, since all the boy had were the ones he'd been wearing at the accident. What size did Joey wear? What were his favorite colors? What were hers?

He wanted to hear her voice again. He wanted to know her, this remarkable woman who'd raised such a remarkable child.

"Mr. McNeal? Visiting time is over."

His attention snapped back. "I'm leaving, Diane."

Rick frowned as he walked past the nurses' station. What was happening to him? He hadn't had this kind of interest in anything since Stacy died, much less another person...much less a woman.

With his hand on the door exiting ICU, he glanced back again at Kate's cubicle. All he could see were the machines keeping her alive.

And that was his only interest in her. Keeping her alive. For Joey.

He had no interest in Kate Burnett as a woman. That part of him died with Stacy.

Satisfied with the explanation, he shoved open the door and left.

"There you are!"

The secretary's exclamation brought Rick to a halt just inside the door of Data Enterprises, the computer software company he'd started ten years ago. "What's wrong?"

"What's wrong?" Judy rose from her desk and set her hands on her hips. "You don't show up until almost ten and you ask what's wrong?"

"Is that Rick?" Chester Bradon, his second in command, came out of his office and stalked down the short hall, followed by the other four programmers. "Where the hell have you been?"

"Has the network crashed?"

"Of course not."

"Bugs in the Claiborne database?"

"There's always bugs," Chester spat. "We'll find them and get rid of them like we always do. That's not the problem."

Rick closed the door. "What is it, then?"

"You're always in the office before everybody. Hours before. With the coffee made and the day's work half done."

Rick faced his staff, all of whom regarded him with varying degrees of worry or irritation. "You all have keys."

"Yeah, but we haven't had to use them since—" Chester broke off and stuck his chin in the air like he always did when he'd put his foot in his mouth...or almost had. "Well, in three years. Charlene is the only one who had hers with her. And she had to dig for ten minutes in that monstrous purse of hers before she found it."

Their worry touched Rick. "Doesn't the boss have the right to be late once in a while?"

They glanced around at each other, knowing he was right but not ready to give up their pique.

"You could've left a voice mail or something," Judy said finally.

"You're right. I should've." He just hadn't had time to think about it, what with getting Joey up and to his mother's in time to make it to the hospital for the short hour visitors were allowed in ICU. "I guess I should tell you now, then, that I'll be late every day for a while. A few weeks, maybe. I'll also be gone in the early afternoon for a couple of hours, and will be leaving right at five."

They all looked at him as if he'd suddenly turned into one of the dragons in the game they worked on in their "spare" time.

"Why?" Ahmed blurted out.

Rick almost smiled. Computer nerds were not known for their social skills. Knowing they'd find out eventually, he gave them a brief outline of the accident and aftermath.

"Ohmigosh," Judy breathed. "It's almost like what happened with..."

Rick's face froze. His staff knew him too well. "Don't all of you have work to do?"

Kate drifted in a painless, timeless realm, divided into two parts—the darkness and The Voice.

At first The Voice was just a soothing interlude between periods of darkness. She'd sunk so deep into a chasm of healing that she couldn't understand what he was saying, didn't even understand that The Voice was forming words and that words conveyed meaning.

Then, one time, she caught a word she understood—Joey. After that she began to listen.

At first she could only pick out a word here and there—mostly her son's name. Then she realized that if she concentrated very hard, she could at least get the gist of what The Voice was telling her. He reassured her that Joey was doing fine, then he would tell her what her son would be doing or what he'd done that day.

"Come back from wherever you are, Kate," The Voice would say. "Joey needs you, and I need to know you'll be okay."

She wanted to do as he asked, wanted to please The Voice. But the darkness still had its strong, warm arms wrapped tightly around her, keeping her from crossing the threshold where the pain began.

Gradually she began rising from the darkness before The Voice began speaking, before she even felt his presence. She would wait expectantly below the threshold, listening for the steps bringing him to her.

Kate knew the time was coming when she'd have to leave her comfortable cocoon, to cross the threshold. But she also knew The Voice would keep her and Joey safe until she felt strong enough to face the pain.

She didn't know how she knew. She didn't question the hows or whys. The knowing was strong, and knowing was all that was important.

The periods Kate spent in the deepest darkness slowly grew shorter. During the time spent waiting for The Voice, she became aware of other activity around her—the low hum of machines, other distant voices that weren't important enough to listen to.

When The Voice arrived, however, she concentrated on him.

It was during one of his visits that she suddenly became aware of the things he wasn't saying. She could hear anguish beneath his words, and knew she was causing him pain.

Remorse mixed with fear.

She didn't want to keep causing The Voice pain, but in order to stop she would have to face the pain herself.

Kate tried to find the courage to cross the threshold, but before she could, The Voice said, "See you tomorrow."

That was always the last thing he said before he went away. Either that or "See you tonight."

She had a reprieve.

Still, she wanted him to know she was trying.

With all her being, she concentrated on forming the words *I'll see you tomorrow.*

Rick halted at the door and looked back at the bed.

Did that low moan come from Kate? What did it mean?

Two steps took him back to her bedside. He waited breathlessly for several long minutes, but she made no sound, moved no muscle on her own.

He sighed in self-disgust and turned away.

Nothing. It meant nothing—except perhaps that he was going crazy. He only thought he heard her voice. He was desperate to believe she was going to be okay, and it comforted him to think she was trying to communicate.

She'd been in a coma for nearly two weeks and had shown no sign of waking. If he let himself think tomorrow would be different, he would just be in for more disappointment.

He turned toward the exit, turning his mind to something that hadn't disappointed him—going home to Joey. He dropped the boy off at Alice's every morning before he went to the hospital. Then, after visiting Kate after work, he picked Joey up and took him home.

Sometimes they ate supper with Alice, sometimes they went to the mall or a movie, sometimes they heated up a can of soup at home. But whatever they did, the hours they spent together were fun.

Fun was something Rick hadn't had in a long, long time.

Kate Burnett needed to wake up…before he got used to having fun.

The first time Kate crossed the threshold was in the still of the night. The low hum of the machines was all she could sense around her, with the occasional sound of a human voice at a distance.

The darkness was no longer insistent that she return, so she'd been hovering just below the threshold ever since The Voice left.

Finally she found the courage to try.

With a deep mental breath, she surfaced.

Ice picks stabbed through her left temple. What had seemed to be the low hum of machines was a ear-splitting cacophony of bleeps and bells. Every muscle ached, every breath burned.

Quickly she dove back beneath the threshold.

Was being conscious worth all the pain?

The answer came quickly. Joey needed her. The Voice needed her, too.

Slowly, cautiously, she surfaced again. Knowing the level of pain she would face helped her to endure several long minutes of consciousness.

Breathing deeply, she took stock of her condition.

True movement was beyond her, but she could twitch muscles in her arms and legs, toes and fingers. Her left arm and leg seemed to be bound, in some way, but she could feel them.

As she became accustomed to the pain, she realized that not every muscle hurt, just those down the left side. The reason every breath burned was that there were tubes of some kind attached to her nose and mouth, and one was lodged in her throat.

Everything wasn't normal, but at least she could feel every part of her body. Satisfied she was going to be okay, Kate sank below the threshold for one last reprieve before she had to face the needles and The Voice at the same time.

Chapter Three

The Voice was coming. It was time.

A small part of Kate hated to leave the comforting, healing darkness—especially knowing what she had to face. But mostly she was eager to know The Voice, to thank him for taking care of Joey, for giving her time to heal.

Through the muffled cushion of the threshold, she heard his footsteps draw nearer, then stop at the edge of her bed.

"Good morning, Kate. Here's your morning kiss from Joey."

She felt warm pressure against her cheek, making her realize she was closer to the surface than she thought.

"How are you doing today?"

She sensed a wary expectancy in his voice, something she hadn't heard before.

"I brought you some flowers. You can't see them or touch them, I know. But I thought perhaps you could smell them and know we were thinking..." His voice turned away on a sigh. "Here. I'll set them on the nightstand beside you. It's a half dozen pink roses."

Pink roses were her favorite.

"I had to call several florists before I found roses with a strong scent. I read it helps to stimulate all of your senses. Anyway, I bought pink instead of red because—I don't know—you seem like a pink rose kind of woman."

The desire to see them was so strong, Kate popped above the threshold before she could make the decision to cross.

She sucked in a quick breath at the first wave of pain. The temptation to dive back below was strong, then she remembered the roses. She couldn't see flowers in the darkness.

Unaware that she'd surfaced, The Voice talked about a trip to the zoo that Joey and Alice were planning for the afternoon. Kate let the deep sounds wash over her as she came to terms with the pain.

Finally it receded enough to be bearable.

"...where the big cats roam around open areas. Lions, cheetahs, panthers. Of course, the big draw in Cat Country is the tigers, since that's the mascot of the university here. But I'm sure you heard about the University of Memphis in Jackson. It's only seventy miles away, after all."

The Voice rambled on, telling her about the university where he'd earned his degree, then went back to talking about the zoo animals Joey would see. He just talked, unaware that she was aware.

Her lips twitched in her first attempt at a smile, though it was hampered by the plastic tube in her mouth, which extended down her throat.

Had he been doing this all along? Talking aimlessly about whatever came to mind?

Yes. Now that she thought about it, she remembered him talking on and on. Well, not remembered, exactly. It was more a feeling...a knowing that came from deep inside her.

Where did the knowing come from? She'd only been conscious a few minutes. And why was The Voice talking so much when he didn't know her?

In hopes something he said interested her enough to wake her.

She knew that, too—though again, didn't know how.

What a sweet, patient man. And she knew he was determined she come out of the darkness. She knew...

There was that word again.

If she'd just awakened, how did she *know* he was sweet?

Suddenly, the full weight of consciousness hit her.

She couldn't possibly know anything about this man. She'd been unconscious for— She had no idea how long she'd been unconscious, but unconscious people were... well, unconscious.

Yet somehow there were things she did know. She knew he visited several times every day. She knew he'd been at the accident. She knew he and his mother were taking care of Joey. She even knew his mother's name—Alice.

But she didn't know how she knew. She didn't know why he was doing any of those things. She didn't even know his name.

Suddenly it was imperative to communicate with him...to see him.

Though she'd been conscious for a few moments the night before, she hadn't yet opened her eyes. So it took an enormous effort. Her eyelids felt as if they weighed a ton apiece. But finally she opened them to slits.

Kate's first impression of The Voice was *big*. He towered above her, with wide shoulders and a muscled chest stretching the blue knit of a golf shirt.

He used his hands as he talked about the orangutans playing on their swing—hands that had long fingers and broad palms. He had a strong face with a square jaw, high cheekbones and well-formed lips that never stopped moving. Thick, dark, close-cropped hair topped everything.

Kate was not surprised that The Voice was big. She'd seen him before, hadn't she? Yes...at the accident.

What did surprise her was how attractive he was...and how much he looked like Joey.

Who was this man? Why was he here? Why was he

taking care of her son? And why had he spent so much time coming to see her?

She opened her mouth to ask, but could barely choke out a sound around the tube stuck down her throat. However, the tiny noise she managed to emit was enough to cut The Voice off midword. His shocked gaze dropped to hers, which let her see the velvet darkness of his brown eyes.

"Kate?" He leaned closer. "Your eyes are open. You're awake. You're okay. Aren't you? Say something!"

She started to complain about him not letting her get a word in edgewise, but again, the only sound she could make was a weak croak deep in her throat.

He ran to the door of her room. "Help! Diane, come *now*. She woke up."

He returned and covered her hand with his. "Thank God. Thank *you* for waking up. Finally I can give Joey wonderful news."

A second later a young redhead appeared beside him. "Ms. Burnett? Please nod if you understand me."

Kate dropped her chin, though it wouldn't go far.

The nurse leaned over the bed and lifted both of Kate's eyelids.

The ice picks stabbed deeper with the increased light. Kate fought the nurse weakly and tried to complain, but still couldn't manage more than a squeak.

"Can you take the tube out?" The Voice asked. "She can't talk with it in."

The young woman shook her head. "I can't extubate without a doctor's orders. Let me call Dr. Lowry. He'll want to come in and see our awakened Sleeping Beauty for himself, at any rate." The nurse grinned at The Voice as if something had just occurred to her. "Prince Charming must've kissed the princess."

The flush that suddenly stained The Voice's cheeks was so surprising and endearing, Kate had to smile, but all her lips managed to do was tug at the tape across them.

"Well, yes, I...but not...'" He cleared his throat. "I give her a kiss every time I come. They're from Joey."

"Uh-huh." With a big smile the nurse moved toward the door. "Sure."

"It never woke her before," he called after her. Then he turned a serious expression to Kate. "Joey wanted me to give you a kiss. He asks me every day if I did."

He was so cute, as embarrassed as a little boy caught kissing a girl by his friends.

"I don't want you to think I've been taking advantage of you."

Since she couldn't talk, Kate blinked to tell him she understood.

He peered at her oddly, as if she'd said something he didn't quite believe. Then he smiled wryly, his left eyebrow lifting. "I suppose we *could* always use the old 'blink once for yes, twice for no' method of communication. But I think we'll have the tube out pretty quick. At least, we will if I have anything to say about it. I've earned the reputation around here for being—how should I put this?—a squeaky wheel."

He'd understood her blink.

Kate wished her mind wasn't so muddled. She knew there was something wrong with this picture, but she couldn't quite pin down what.

The Voice peered in the direction of the door. "Looks as if I don't have to squeak at the moment. She's already on her way back."

The nurse entered seconds later. "Dr. Lowry is in the hospital. He'll be here in a few minutes. Which means you have to leave."

The Voice was clearly affronted. "Leave? Now? She's finally conscious. I want to talk to her."

"We've had this discussion before. There are things we may have to do that can be somewhat undignified for the patient. It's best for everyone if there's no family hanging around." She pointed at the door. "Go."

Kate blinked again, involuntarily this time. *Family?*

"I'll leave, but I'll be in the ICU waiting room. Come get me as soon as you're through doing what you and Dr. Lowry need to do, okay?"

"It might take a while. Go get some breakfast and a cup of coffee across the street. You look as if you could use nourishment."

Rick set his chin. "I'll be in the ICU waiting room."

As he left, the nurse shook her head. "How do you put up with such a stubborn man?"

Put up with him? Why would she have to put up with him?

The nurse, Diane, pulled the curtains across the windows looking out into the hall. "Oh, well. I guess it's a good thing he's stubborn. He makes certain you're getting the best of care, grilling whichever doctor is on duty about your condition and generally driving the nurses crazy. He hasn't missed a single visiting time yet. He's the first one through the door, and we have to shoo him out at least once a day."

Kate knew he'd visited, but it surprised her to learn that he'd come so often and stayed so long. The Voice wasn't family, or even a friend. Not even a casual acquaintance. Why would he visit so faithfully?

As the nurse moved around the bed, checking on wires and machines, she continued. "He talks to you the whole time he's here. Mostly about your son. Probably hoping it would bring you around. I guess it worked, didn't it? I saw Joey when you were first brought in. The spitting image of his father, isn't he? He was so cute, fast asleep on his dad's lap."

Spitting image of his *father?*

Kate closed her eyes. What the heck was going on?

"Everything looks fine. The doctor will be here any second." Diane paused by the bed. "He's kind of cute, though. Your husband, I mean, not Dr. Lowry. Or is he your ex-husband? Or boyfriend?"

Kate's eyes opened wide, then quickly narrowed against the light.

Diane grinned. "I have to tell you, the nursing staff is speculating wildly as to why he has a different last name. Especially since all he'll say is that it's a long story. We sniff romance in there someplace, and we do love romance." Her green eyes twinkled. "Anyway, you're a lucky woman to have a man who cares about you so much."

A man who cared about her? Husband? Kate didn't even know The Voice's name.

She let her eyes close as she tried to make sense of the nurse's statements. But she was so tired, nothing made sense.

Being awake was exhausting.

She fought sleep, however, afraid she'd slip back into the darkness.

The doctor poking and prodding, pulling out tubes and asking questions, helped. But when he left, she could fight it no longer.

Perhaps it would be best to let the darkness reclaim her.

She'd obviously wakened in a parallel universe. Maybe next time she'd wake in the right one.

Rick stood in the door to Kate's room, watching her sleep. He held on to the steel doorjamb to keep from rushing in and shaking her, to make certain she hadn't gone back into her coma.

Diane had assured him she was only sleeping. Still…the need to see for himself was strong.

The thick tube was gone from her mouth, and she was breathing softly, evenly on her own. The sheets were tucked tightly around her. Her arms lay on top, the left one still splinted.

Rick was beside the bed before he'd made a conscious decision to move. Kate Burnett drew him like flowers drew butterflies. He hadn't been away from the office this much in years. Since Stacy died, to be exact.

What was wrong with him? Was he attracted to Kate? How was that possible? She'd been unconscious the whole time he'd known her, except for the few minutes at the accident scene when he'd been too busy worrying about keeping her alive to notice anything else.

Besides, he could never forget Stacy. His wife. His first and only love.

The reason he came was because Kate seemed so fragile, so vulnerable. She needed him to take care of her until she could take care of herself again. She was no different from Joey in that way. Both of them needed his help.

It felt good to help someone again, to be needed. He'd been lonely since Stacy died, felt useless.

What was the harm in helping them, when everyone benefited? He would take care of Kate and Joey Burnett, get them back on their feet, then he would happily send them on their way.

Perhaps by then the chasm left in his life by Stacy's death would be healed. Perhaps by then he'd feel like living again.

Unaccustomed to the lighter form of sleep, Kate wasn't far under, and when she sensed a presence nearby that needed her, her mother alarm blared.

Instead of Joey, however, The Voice stood by her bed. His dark eyes were unfocused, faraway, troubled.

Though she didn't know this man and certainly didn't know what worried him, she wanted to ease his burden. But she couldn't help without knowing what caused his troubles.

At least she could distract him. "Hello."

Her throaty word startled The Voice from his thoughts, and he focused on her face. "Hi. I didn't mean to wake you."

"You…didn't." Her voice was hoarse and hesitant.

Concern returned to his face. "Are you in pain? Should I call the nurse?"

She shook her head and grimaced. "I'm…okay."

He nodded, but didn't seem convinced.

Since she didn't know how else to distract him, she decided to satisfy her own burning need for information.

"What—" her mouth kept going dry, and she had to swallow "—your name."

He blinked in surprise. "Oh. I guess you don't know who I am, do you? Odd. Seems like I've known you for…" He sighed. "My name is Rick McNeal."

"You were…accident?"

"Yes." He glanced over his shoulder, then back at her. "How much do you remember?"

Kate let her eyes close as she recalled topping a hill just blocks from the new apartment and rear-ending a Jeep. The moments after the initial impact were a blur of spinning and rolling, glass shattering and metal crunching…and pain.

"I'm sorry," he said. "We shouldn't talk about this until you're stronger."

Kate opened her eyes. "I want…to know."

He frowned. "I don't know how much I should tell you now. Do you remember being hit?"

She nodded.

"Afterward?"

"You…pulled us…out."

"Yes. You asked me to take care of Joey for you. Do you remember that?"

Kate thought back. Had she asked him? She'd always been the type of person who wouldn't ask a friend to lend her a pen until she'd dug through her purse and concluded there was no other recourse. She hated asking *anyone* for even the smallest favor. To ask a perfect stranger to take care of her son for an indefinite period of time was unthinkable.

Yet…now that he mentioned it, she remembered she'd

not only asked this man to take care of Joey—she'd begged him. She'd been desperate to keep her son out of the clutches of the state child care system. She would've pleaded with the devil himself, having experienced the foster care system firsthand.

There was no way they were going to get their unfeeling, red-taped hands around *her* child.

Kate nodded again. "Is he...okay?"

"He's fine. Don't you worry a second about Joey. My mother takes good care of him during the day and loves every minute of it."

Kate uttered words it had always galled her to say. "Thank you."

He waved away her gratitude. "Taking care of your son has been a joy, trust me. Both for myself and my mother. It's helped us... Well, one soul baring at a time."

"Soul...baring?"

He gazed at her with a worried frown. "If the nurses know, they won't let me see you."

"Know...what?"

Rick glanced over his shoulder again. Finally, he took a deep breath and said, "I'm the man you ran into. The man responsible for—" he swept his arm across her "—all this."

His words confused her. She ran into the back of him, didn't she? That meant the accident was her fault. Yet he clearly blamed himself.

She frowned. "You stopped...on purpose?"

She had the impression he was a nurturing man, not a reckless driver.

Again the peculiarity of her thought struck her. Where did these "impressions" come from? The fanciful dreams of an unconscious mind?

Yet...he had to be a nurturing man. He was taking care of Joey, after all. And he was taking care of her.

"God, no!" His face tightened. "There was a kid on a bike, and I slammed on my brakes. But then I just sat there in a daze when I should've been getting the hell out of the road. Then you came over the hill and couldn't avoid hitting me. Then the Cadillac slammed into you. I can't tell you how sorry I am.''

She swallowed. This man seemed as if he needed a little nurturing, too.

Kate's frown deepened. Another insight into The Voice's psyche. She hadn't felt this kind of connection with anyone but Joey in a long, long time. She'd cut herself off, protected herself from such intimacy. Connections created dependence, and when you depended on another person for something, they always expected to be repaid—in one way or another.

So why did she wish she had the strength to put her arms around him and kiss his troubles away?

''Are you in pain?''

A light touch made her lift her eyes. He leaned close to her, his face taut with concern. His concern was genuine. She felt it as clearly as she felt the ice pick stabbing her left eye.

Another connection.

Kate closed her eyes on a wince, because she didn't have the strength to fight it any other way.

''Kate, please. Are you in pain?''

She didn't say anything and didn't open her eyes.

He took her nonreply as a yes, because he raised his voice. ''Diane! She's hurting. Help her. Please.''

Kate opened her eyes in time to see the nurse hurry in.

Diane took one look at Kate, then turned on Rick. ''I said you could only come in if you promised not to wake her.''

''I didn't. I was just standing here and she woke up.''

''Uh-huh.''

''I swear I didn't touch her or say anything.''

''Whatever.'' The nurse walked around the bed to the IV. ''She needs rest now, more than anything. You'll have to leave.''

"Already?"

"She's weak and in pain. She can only take small doses of visitors."

He sighed heavily. "Okay. I'm sorry. The last thing I want to do is set her back."

"I know you're excited that she's out of the coma," the nurse said kindly. "But you still have to leave."

The Voice shrugged into a light jacket. No, he had a name now. Rick McNeal.

"When can I bring Joey?"

"I knew you'd ask, so I asked Dr. Lowry. Tonight, but just for a minute."

Rick nodded, then glanced at Kate. He must've noticed her open eyes because he smiled. "Did you hear that? Joey's going to be bouncing off the walls until then."

Kate smiled. She was going to get to see her sweet baby boy. He must be scared to death with all that had happened, and having to live with strangers.

"You'd better let him, then," Diane said firmly. "He needs to get it out of his system before he gets here."

"I'll take him to the park before we come. Wears him out every time."

A pang gripped Kate's heart. Rick McNeal already knew her son well enough to know how to sap Joey's enormous store of energy.

"See you later, Kate." He bent over and placed another kiss on her cheek. "Thank you for waking up."

The last words were said very quietly, next to her ear. Their intimacy caused a shiver to run through her.

He missed it because Diane caught his attention with teasing words. "Is that kiss from Joey, too?"

Rick grinned. "Half of it."

"Off with you. Now."

"Okay, I'm going."

"Goodbye," Kate whispered.

Rick stopped and turned. Did he hear her? "I'll see you tonight."

His gaze was intense, and the words echoed from someplace deep inside. She'd heard them before.

He sent her a warm, intimate smile.

As he turned to leave, she almost caught the elusive trail that would lead her to the source of the connection.

She let her eyes close.

There was that word again. Connections. Knowings. Words. Words. Words. It was all too much for a muddled brain to handle.

"Go back to sleep, honey," the nurse said quietly.

Sleep. Yes, that's what she needed. She'd already discovered it wasn't quite the darkness, but it was close.

"Rick!"

Joey's cry brought Alice's head around. "What are you doing here in the middle of the day?"

He grinned. "I have some news."

Since Joey had run to him, Rick lifted the boy high in the air. "You ready for some good news, little guy?"

Joey giggled at the rough play, then when Rick set him on the floor, he looked up with barely contained excitement. "Is it about my mommy?"

"It sure is."

His blue eyes widened. "Is she awake? Can I see her?"

"She sure is and you sure can. Tonight. How about that?"

The boy squealed in delight as he took a running, jumping, twirling turn around the room.

Alice beamed at the boy. "Did she say anything?"

"Did she ask about me?" Joey asked.

"Yes, she did." Rick sat on the couch next to his mother and pulled Joey onto his lap. "She's worried about you. That's why I'm going to take you to see her tonight. But you have to be good as gold. Understand? She's been hurt, and you have to treat her like…like a toy that's been broken and you're afraid will break again if you treat it rough."

"Can I give her a hug?" The boy was worried, but Rick wanted to impress on him the importance of behaving.

"I don't know. We'll have to see how she feels. The nurse said she has to take things slow and easy, and we're sticking to that. Okay?"

Joey nodded solemnly. "'Kay, Rick. If I can see Mommy, I'll be gold good...promise."

Rick smiled at Alice over the boy's head as he gave him a hug. "I know you will, little guy. Just remember...slow and easy."

The smell of roses was the first thing Kate became aware of when she woke—after the pain, of course. The scent made her realize she'd yet to see them.

The doctor had told her to limit movement for the next twenty-four hours, especially her head. So she turned very slowly, very carefully until the flowers came into view. Half a dozen delicate pink roses were arranged in a clear vase with baby's breath and greenery. They were just out of the bud stage, barely open.

Tears stung her eyes. Rick McNeal had gone to a lot of trouble to bring her the roses.

Well, maybe calling several florists wasn't *a lot* of trouble, but it was more than anyone had done for her before. She didn't know this man, and he didn't know her, but he'd bought her pink roses with a scent hoping the smell would draw her out of her coma.

Pink roses. How in the world did he know they were her favorite?

Connections.

The word popped into her head, making her frown and turn away.

There was *no* connection. This link she felt with Rick McNeal had to be a bizarre dream she'd had while she was unconscious. She had a brain injury, after all. That had to be causing irregularities in her thinking patterns.

Still...pink roses.

Pain twinged down the left side of her face as she frowned.

A coincidence, that's all. Or, more likely, Joey had told him what she liked.

As if she could conjure her son by thinking of him, she heard his voice.

"I'm here to see my mommy," Joey proudly announced.

Kate smiled. Her baby. It had been ages since she'd seen him.

The Voice—no, Rick—said something, more quietly, that she couldn't quite hear. Odd. Somehow she knew that even if she didn't hear his voice again for fifty years, she'd recognize it.

"She's been asleep," a female voice said. "Let me see if she's awake."

An older nurse entered Kate's room and smiled. "You have visitors."

Kate smiled weakly. "I heard."

The nurse turned. "Ten minutes. That's it."

They must've been standing at the door, because they came right in, though Kate could see only Rick. Joey was below bed level.

"Mommy!"

"Whoa, partner." Rick caught her son. "Slow and easy, remember?"

"I want to give her a kiss," Joey complained.

Rick lifted him.

Joey twisted in his arms, and she finally saw his face. He looked healthy and happy and excited to see her. Amazingly, he also looked so much like Rick, he could be the man's clone...or son. Except for his eyes. Joey had blue eyes, several shades darker than hers.

Still, it was no wonder all the nurses thought Rick was Joey's father.

He held out his small arms. "Mommy!"

Though it hurt to smile, Kate couldn't stop. "My baby. Oh, it's good to see you."

She lifted her right arm, but was so weak she could only manage to reach his foot. He had on a brand new pair of athletic shoes. Expensive ones.

"Joey, I'm going to lower you so you can give your mom a kiss, but you have to promise to be very gentle and very quiet, okay?" Rick said.

Joey went still in Rick's arms. "Yes, sir."

Slowly Rick dipped the boy toward her.

As Joey placed a gentle kiss on her cheek, Kate ran her fingers through her son's thick silky hair, tears stinging her eyes again. "I love you, Joey."

"I love you, too, Mommy."

She kissed his velvet cheek just before Rick lifted him away. Her son smelled of soap and… "Are you…wearing cologne?"

As Rick settled Joey on his right arm so the boy could see her, Joey slipped one small arm around Rick's neck and rubbed his chin with his other hand, like a man feeling his whiskers. "Aftershave. Rick gave me some."

"You smell good," she murmured, but the image bothered her.

A young boy watching a man shave and wanting to be like him was normal. But the scene implied an intimacy, a caring, close association that only she had shared with her son. A father/son intimacy—something she could never give him.

Joey was getting to the age when he would need a man in his life. She'd planned to find an older man, a grandfather figure who would take him fishing, now and then, and do other guy things with him.

"When you coming home, Mommy?" Joey asked.

"Home?" For the first time, Kate realized they had no home.

She and Joey had just arrived in Memphis from Jackson, Tennessee, where she'd quit her job as a bookkeeper for a small manufacturing firm. She'd found an apartment in the Memphis newspaper the Sunday before, but hadn't yet signed the lease. How long would the resident manager give her before she rented the apartment to someone else?

Which brought up a more pressing question.

She shifted her gaze to Rick. "How long...have I been here?"

"Almost two weeks," he said.

"Two...?" Foreboding settled in her stomach like a lead weight.

Forget the apartment. She was supposed to have started a new job on the Monday after they'd moved to town. Would her new employer have found someone else when she hadn't shown up?

If they hadn't already, they would soon. They hadn't had someone in over a month who could so much as pull a financial statement, and they had been getting desperate to get their books straight. Tax time was closing in.

Kate couldn't even lift her hand, much less sit up. There was no way she could work at a computer all day. Not for several more weeks, at the soonest.

She felt as if she were choking. She wasn't going to have a job when she got out of the hospital—if they ever let her out. And since she was in between jobs, she was in between insurance coverage. How was she going to pay the bill?

Rick shifted Joey in his arms. "What's wrong?"

"I just realized..." Her gaze shifted to Joey.

The boy's small body tightened in the man's arms. "Mommy?"

"It's okay, baby," she said quickly. "Everything's going...to be okay."

Joey relaxed immediately. He'd heard her words before. A comfort phrase from mother to son.

Rick wasn't as easy to convince. "What's wrong, Kate?"

"I can't..."

"Can't what?"

She couldn't do a lot of things. She couldn't pay the enormous hospital bill she was running up. She couldn't take care of her son. She couldn't move. But mostly, she couldn't talk about her troubles in front of Joey.

Rick's wide, warm hand covered hers. "Don't worry, Kate. I'm taking care of Joey, and I'll take care of you. Everything's going to be okay."

Kate closed her eyes. The phrase he threw back in her face was anything but comforting. She hated taking help from anyone.

When people helped you, they felt you owed them. And they always expected to be paid back tenfold.

Her gaze traveled up the man towering over her bed, her son clasped tightly in his arms.

What would Rick McNeal expect as payment?

Chapter Four

"You ate every bite." The twenty-something nurse beamed at Kate three days later. "Dr. Lowry said that if you're doing as well this morning as you did yesterday, he's going to put you in a regular room."

Kate smiled weakly. At least she wouldn't be going into debt at such a rapid rate.

"Are you tired, honey? Would you like me to put the bed down?"

"Maybe just a little," Kate said. "But please not all the way. My eyes don't hurt so much when I don't have to look directly up at the lights."

"I'll dim them." The nurse smiled sympathetically as she turned down the lights, then lowered the head of the bed until Kate was half sitting, half reclining. "Do you want something stronger for the pain?"

"It's not so bad today."

She closed her eyes as the nurse walked out with the tray and listened to the strong, steady blip of the heart monitor. The better she became physically, the worse she felt.

She didn't know how much all this intense hospital care

was going to cost, but she'd been in ICU for over two weeks. The bill had to be astronomical already, and it was growing with every heartbeat.

A dollar a heartbeat, the heart monitor had been saying ever since she realized her predicament.

But she had no money, no job, no place to live...and a son to raise.

Kate shivered and pulled the covers up over her shoulders.

She was so tired. Tired of lying here hour after hour. Tired of the pain. Tired of fighting for survival, for every dollar that came her way. Tired of feeling so alone.

Tired. So tired.

With a ragged sigh, she settled deeper into the pillow.

"Hello, beautiful lady."

The low tones couldn't disguise the deep-throated voice. The familiar, comforting sound plus a feather touch on her cheek brought Kate from the doze she'd slipped into to escape her depression. She opened her eyes to see Rick's darkly handsome face pulling away.

Had he kissed her?

Her smile was uncertain, her voice raspy from sleep. "Hi."

"Oh. Hello." His face was so serious, so concerned. "Sorry. I didn't mean to wake you."

"I wasn't really asleep. Besides, you're the only thing I have to break the monotony of lying here hour after hour."

His features finally relaxed into a smile, though a wry one. "Glad I'm good for something."

"I'm sure you're good for other things, too."

When he raised a brow, Kate realized her words might've sounded flirtatious. But they weren't meant that way...were they?

No. Definitely not.

Then she recalled the first words he'd said, the words which woke her.

Hello, beautiful lady.

Up until now she hadn't given a single thought to her appearance. Now that she did, she realized she must look like a prize fighter at the end of ten hard-fought rounds.

Her right hand—the hand not sticking out the end of a cast—automatically went to her hair. Dear God! It hadn't been washed since... And this absolutely gorgeous man had been looking at her since...

She winced, both for her embarrassment and because of it. She couldn't remember the last time she cared what a man thought of her appearance. And this man *wasn't* gorgeous. Of course, he wasn't plain, either—

"Is your head hurting?" Rick asked.

"What? Oh. Maybe a little. But I'm feeling better every day. I just realized I must look like a witch. My hair hasn't been washed since the accident and..." Her hand touched the left side of her head. "I'm bald!"

He reached across the bed to the half-inch hairs sticking from the left side of her head like a punk rocker's with too much freeze-spray. "Don't worry, it'll grow back. Besides, you're only half-bald." His touch was light, almost reverent. "You have beautiful hair, you know. The color of moonlight."

"Beautiful?" Her eyes narrowed. "I would tell you to pull my other leg, but since it's broken in four places, it would probably be painful."

His face brightened. "A joke! You *are* feeling better."

Kate frowned. His obvious pleasure created a corresponding blossom of pleasure in her. Not a good sign. Since Mitch's desertion, pleasing a man had dropped way down on her list of priorities—about two lines below cleaning under the refrigerator. "I'm not joking. If you think I'm beautiful, you must not get out much. And when you do, you must not go anywhere but prize fights."

"Another joke! This is fantastic."

There it was again, a tiny twinge of pleasure at pleasing him. "I'm not—"

"I know, I know, you're not joking." He picked up her one good hand and held it between his own very large, very warm ones. "I'm not, either, Kate. Okay, your hair isn't ready for a photo shoot. But after all I've been through and all you've been through, the mere fact that you're breathing makes you beautiful to me."

A gentle tug was all it took for Kate to pull her hand from his. "You don't know me. There's no reason you should care if I'm breathing or not."

"I do know you," he said softly. "I see you every minute I spend with Joey."

Suddenly overcome with emotion, Kate closed her eyes to hide it. She couldn't remember the last time anyone but Joey cared whether she breathed or not.

No, that wasn't true. She remembered the last time exactly. It was the day before she learned she was pregnant with Mitch's baby. She'd thought he cared about her, thought he would welcome the child they'd made together.

She'd thought wrong.

Kate dug the ragged fingernails on her right hand into her palm, willing the years-old pain away. She didn't care anymore. Mitch's desertion, his rejection of his own child, couldn't touch her anymore. She'd made a life for herself and Joey. They didn't need anyone else.

They didn't need Rick McNeal, and she certainly didn't care what he thought of her appearance.

Still, she was going to wash her hair as soon as they'd let her.

"Kate, are you—"

"Where's Joey?" she asked over his concern. Concern might make her believe he cared. Concern was a lie.

"He's at Mom's. I'll bring him by this evening."

"It isn't evening?" She didn't bother glancing toward the windows because there were none. ICU was apparently buried in the bowels of the hospital.

"No. I'm on my lunch hour."

Kate frowned. More evidence of his concern. "I'm taking up so much of your time. You don't have to come as often as—''

''Yes, I do.'' His warm hand swallowed hers once again. ''Don't worry a single moment about my time. I don't have anything else to do except work. And I've been doing too much of that the past three years.''

She shouldn't ask. Personal questions implied concern on her end, and concern meant she cared. But she wanted to know. ''Why?''

''Oh, lots of reasons.'' He frowned. ''Your hand is like ice.'' He took it between both of his and rubbed vigorously.

''It's cold in here.''

He nodded as he rubbed. ''They keep it cold to inhibit the growth of germs.''

''Why?''

''They want to inhibit germs to cut down on the risk—''

''I know what germs do. I want to know what you do, and why you've been working so much.'' Realizing how imperious that sounded, she added, ''If it's not too personal.''

''Of course it's not too personal. I own a software company. Data Enterprises. We build custom software programs for businesses.''

''You mean like a database?''

Rick nodded. ''Mostly, but some other applications, too. Some of my people are working on a game in their spare time. They think it's going to make them rich.''

''Joey loves computer games,'' Kate said wistfully.

''I know.''

She frowned. He knew entirely too much about her son. ''What makes you say you've been working too much?''

Rick's dark, thick eyebrows nearly touched across the sudden furrow between them. He gently laid her hand on her stomach. ''I guess I've been using work to escape my ghosts.''

''Ghosts?''

He smiled sadly. ''Not literally, though it might seem

that way when I tell you that my wife died three years ago. I've been burying myself in my work because...well, because programming takes all my concentration. Because it lets me forget about Stacy for hours at a stretch.''

His pain vibrated in the air, vivid, acute. It seemed a separate entity from them both, yet part of each one. Part of Rick because of the memories. Part of Kate because he'd touched her heart.

What would it be like...to be loved so deeply? So deeply that three years of separation couldn't dull the pain.

''I'm sorry,'' she told him. And she was. This kind, caring man deserved to be happy. ''How did she die?''

''She—''

''Hello, Mr. McNeal.''

The cheery voice drew their attention to the doorway.

Rick straightened with what seemed like relief. ''Hello, Diane. I didn't see you when I came in.''

''I was probably in another room.'' She carried a fresh IV bag to the other side of the bed. ''Have you heard the news?''

''What news?'' he asked.

''Our sleeping beauty is moving to a regular room today.''

''She is?'' His happy face beamed down at Kate. ''Why didn't you tell me?''

''I didn't know if it was for sure.''

''It is.'' Diane placed a finger on Kate's wrist. ''Linda talked to Dr. Lowry just a few minutes ago. When she told him how well you're doing, he said to make the arrangements. She's working on it now. Should be just a few hours.''

The nurse lifted her wristwatch to check Kate's pulse.

Rick grinned. ''This is great news. Joey'll go into orbit. Now he can visit anytime. Do you know how long it'll be before she can go home?''

Diane dropped Kate's wrist and wrote a number on her

chart. "Dr. Lowry said probably a few more days, just for observation."

"Did you hear that, Kate? You'll be home in a few days."

Kate nodded, but couldn't speak for the sudden lump in her throat. Home. Did she have a home to go to? Did she have a job?

There was so much to think about, so much to do. She didn't have time to lie in a hospital bed "just for observation."

Yet the very thought of walking out of the hospital, of finding a place to stay and a way to pay for it, made Kate want to sink back into the coma.

"What's wrong?" Rick asked.

She shook her head. "Nothing."

"Don't tell me that," he said quietly but firmly. "You're as pale as you were when they first brought you in."

She studied his face. She never discussed her problems with anyone. "I just realized…"

"What did you realize?" he prompted when she trailed off.

Kate took a deep breath. This was hard. "Joey and I were moving to Memphis that night you ran into me, because I'd just accepted a new job here. I was supposed to start the following Monday."

Rick's frown deepened. "That was almost three weeks ago. Do you think they would've held it for you?"

Kate felt like crying, but she couldn't. Not in front of Rick. "Would you, if a new employee didn't show up for three weeks? Didn't call or anything?"

He winced. "You've got a point. What's the company's name? And the name of your supervisor there? I'll call and let them know what happened to you."

"You don't have to—"

"No, I don't, but I'm going to. You're not in any condition to make calls. I'll do it as soon as I get back to the office. It's possible they haven't hired a replacement yet."

"Possible, but not likely. And it's not as if I can start tomorrow. They're not going to wait God knows how long for me. They were shorthanded as it was."

He shrugged. "You never know."

"You've done so much already. You don't have to—"

"The name, please."

Kate reluctantly gave him the information.

"There's something else, isn't there?" he asked after he'd written the names on a small notebook pulled from a rear pants pocket.

How could he read her so well? Was it possible Rick felt the same kind of connection with her that she'd been feeling with him?

Connections.

That word again.

No. She didn't believe in connections, not this kind. What she felt went beyond psychic phenomena. This was a soul mate bond…and she certainly didn't believe in that.

Did she?

Kate shivered. The possibility was alarming. No one had ever been so close to her.

Yet…having such a connection was enticing. It meant she would no longer be alone.

"Kate?"

She pushed the ridiculous notion away. "Yes. You're right. I had an apartment lined up, too. It was close to work and right around the corner from a day care for Joey. But I hadn't signed the lease."

"So you think they may have rented it to someone else. What was the name of the complex?"

"I'm 99 percent sure they've rented it. There were several other people interested in it. I just happened to get there first."

"The name?"

She sighed again. "Pendleton Forest."

He wrote the name down, then looked up. "What else?"

"Nothing."

"Kate…"

His insistence confused her. She'd always done everything on her own, never asked anyone for help, never shared her problems with anyone. Who cared, after all? "What?"

He pinned her with a hard look. "Are you always this stubborn?"

"Look who's talking."

After a moment's staring contest, Kate gave in with a sigh. Obviously, Rick cared. Why, she didn't know, but she was too tired to argue with him. "I'm just worried, okay?"

"About what?"

"Oh, things like how I'm going to pay for the hospital bill with no insurance and no job. Like how I'm going to find a job. Like when I'm even going to be able to. Like where I'm going to go when they release me, since I have no home."

His face set in grim lines. "You don't have to worry about the hospital bill. That's taken care of. As for where you'll go—"

"How is the hospital taken care of?"

"By me. At least, until the insurance is settled."

"What?" Rick paying her bill had never occurred to her. "Don't be ridiculous. Why would you?"

"The accident was my fault, Kate. Which makes your possibly having no job and losing your apartment my fault."

"How was the accident your fault? I ran into the back of you."

"Which you wouldn't have done if I hadn't been sitting there in the middle of the road. Over a hill, no less."

"Did the police say it was your fault?"

"Well, no. But they didn't take into account the fact that I was dead tired from working a seventy-hour week. If I hadn't been, I would've gotten out of the road."

"It's not your fault."

"Maybe not by the law, but technically I'm at fault. I'm

going to make things right, Kate, so just set your mind to that.''

Kate didn't like it. She'd always been responsible for herself, for her own debts. But how could she argue? She had no money.

"As for where you're going to go when they let you out of the hospital, we'll work it out."

"How?"

"Well, my mother has several spare rooms—"

"No."

His eyes narrowed. "The only other option, then, is my place."

"*Definitely* no."

"That's your favorite word, isn't it?"

Her chin tightened. "I don't take charity."

"It isn't charity, Kate."

"Oh no? Then what is it?"

His chin lifted at her sarcastic tone. "It's paying what I owe. I caused you to be jobless and homeless. I'll take care of you until we rectify the situation."

"I won't go home with you."

"Then where will you go?" he asked mercilessly. "Do you have another option available to you? A friend in town? Family?"

"No. I have nobody. You know that." Kate struggled to sit straight. His looming over her felt like he had all the power. Between the brace on her arm and leg and the reclining position of the bed, however, she couldn't.

"What on earth are you doing?"

"I'm trying to sit up!"

"Well, why didn't you say something?" He placed a hand under each of her armpits and lifted her to a sitting position. "There. Better?"

Kate grabbed the bed rail. It was the first time in weeks she had no support at her back. The sudden weightless feeling made her dizzy. "Oh."

He quickly wrapped an arm around her back to steady her. "Are you okay?"

Just that quickly, his anger dissipated into helpful concern.

Kate allowed herself to lean against his support. Just for a minute. Just until her head cleared.

The solid strength of his arm was reassuring. The faint warm scent emanating from his shirt contrasted sharply with the antiseptic smells of the hospital. It was earthy and masculine and somehow familiar.

He placed a gentle kiss on her forehead. "Beautiful Kate. I'm sorry."

"For what?"

He slowly laid her back against the bed. "For arguing with you. You're not in any condition to sit up, much less make any decisions right now."

"But—"

"Hush now." He smiled with grim satisfaction. "Don't worry. I'll take care of everything."

"No."

"Yes."

Kate sank back into the mattress as he turned to leave.

She had no doubt that he would take care of everything. He seemed adept at taking over people's lives.

She should call him back, tell him to go away, that he'd done enough.

Instead, she closed her eyes. She was so very tired. And it was all too easy to let him take charge…for the moment. She could argue about it later.

She wouldn't let herself or Joey become accustomed to his help, though. Help disappeared when you needed it most.

Rick shook his head as he pushed the elevator button.

Stubborn woman. What did Kate expect to do? Walk out of the hospital and go job hunting? She couldn't even sit on her own, much less walk with the confidence needed to land a job.

What else could she do but go to his apartment or his mother's? It wasn't charity. It was the least he could do.

Rick hit the lit elevator button again.

It was obvious she couldn't take care of herself. Why wouldn't she let him help her? She didn't have anyone. She needed him, and he needed to know she was going to be okay. He could no more say goodbye to her at the hospital door than he could've handed Joey over to the state child authorities.

Joey. Rick could see now where the boy learned his independent ways. Being self-sufficient was a good quality, but if Kate wasn't careful, Joey was going to end up thinking he didn't need anyone, either. He'd end up a social recluse, like...

Like Rick had been for the past three years.

About to call for the elevator again, Rick stopped with his finger poised over the already lit button.

But that was different. He'd had a reason to avoid people.

So...maybe Kate had a reason, too.

He leaned against the cool marble wall, his arms crossed over his chest.

Had Kate suffered a heart-breaking loss, as he had? Perhaps something to do with Joey's father? He'd asked Joey about his father, but the boy simply said he didn't have one. At the accident Kate said Joey's father was gone.

All the more reason for Rick to help her. He knew how important it was to have someone to lean on. He wanted her to lean on him. In fact, he was going to insist on it.

Who did you have to lean on?

The question seemed to float out of the empty elevator car as the doors slid open.

Startled, Rick almost let the elevator doors close. Jutting a hand between them, he forced them open and stepped inside. As he pushed the ground floor button, he answered the ethereal question. He'd had his mother and a few good friends.

But he hadn't leaned on his friends. He'd avoided them, shunned their offers of companionship. He hadn't heard from any of them in over a year. And his mother had been leaning on him so much since his father died, he hadn't been able to lean on her.

As the elevator dropped to the next floor to pick up another passenger, Rick stared at the rows of numbers, only one of which was lit.

How was he different from Kate?

Not a helluva lot.

So how could he insist that she take his help, when he wouldn't take it from others?

Rick shook his head. His logic didn't make any difference in the way he felt. He needed to help Kate. He needed her to need him, this woman who didn't want to need anyone.

Maybe it was to expiate the guilt he'd wallowed in after Stacy's death. Maybe it was to give what he'd been too buried in remorse to take—the helping hand of a friend. Maybe it was so Joey would have everything a growing boy required.

He didn't know. He only knew that the feeling went soul deep and that when Kate left the hospital, he'd drag her to his mother's house if he had to...for her sake, for Joey's sake and for his own.

Rick pushed open the door to the kitchen, then stood in the doorway, shaking his head.

Joey kneeled backward on the chair facing the window in the breakfast nook, fully dressed. A bowl with a spoon laid carefully across it and a glass lined with a white film of milk testified that he'd already eaten. The wake-up smell of coffee filled the room.

"No matter how early I get up," Rick complained. "You're already up, usually with breakfast fixed."

Joey twisted in his seat. "Want some cereal, Rick?"

"Well, yes, but I'll get it. I've been fixing my own breakfast for many more years than you've been around."

"Want acupa coffee?" the boy asked hopefully.

He was so eager to help, and so damn self-sufficient that Rick's heart twisted. Joey wasn't even five yet, but he could probably survive alone for weeks in a reasonably provisioned house.

On one hand, he wanted to praise Kate for teaching her son responsibility at such a young age. On the other hand, he wanted to shake her. She'd robbed Joey of his childhood, making him an adult long before he needed to be.

"I can get that, too." Rick headed for the coffeemaker. As he reached above it for a mug, he asked, "What's so interesting out the window?"

"Birds. I'm waitin' for Miz Alice," Joey announced. "We're gonna visit Mommy today in a brand-new room. A room for almost-well people."

"Miss Alice..." It was strange calling her that, but she'd insisted on Joey using her first name instead of Mrs. McNeal. "...isn't coming over here. I'm taking you to her house as usual. Visiting hours don't start until ten o'clock."

"She said 'first thing in the mornin'.'"

Rick pulled the half-and-half from the refrigerator. "You'll learn one day that 'first thing in the morning' is a relative term. Especially to women."

Joey's face puckered with confusion. "Relative?"

Rick poured exactly one tablespoon of half-and-half into his coffee. "*Relative* means that the term means something different to everyone."

Joey glanced at the clock on the wall. Amazingly, the boy could read the old-fashioned kind already. "It's only six-thirty 'clock."

Rick mmm-hmmed as he took his first sip of coffee. The scent wafting up his nostrils as the hot liquid spread sharp flavor across his tongue made him sigh with pleasure.

Joey's shoulders slumped as he climbed down from the

chair. "May I play Pokemon on the 'puter while you get ready for work, Rick?"

"You don't want to stay here and talk to me?"

A small shoulder lifted. "You always read the paper."

"I guess I do." Rick smiled. "Sure. Go on up."

Joey pushed on the door. "I'll clean up while you get dressed. 'Kay?"

Rick frowned. He knew without checking that Joey's room was immaculate—his bed made up and his clothes folded neatly in a drawer. "No, it's not okay. I'll clean up. You're a kid, for Pete's sake. Act like one."

Joey's face scrunched with worry. "How?"

Rick's heart melted. If Kate were there, he'd give her three or four pieces of his mind. "Go fire up the computer."

The boy's face cleared. "Okay. See ya upstairs."

Rick frowned into his coffee. How long would it take to teach a kid how to be a kid? And would Joey be around long enough for Rick to find out?

"Mommy? You 'sleep?"

Kate opened her eyes on a wide smile. "Joey! No, baby. I was just resting my eyes."

Joey stood carefully in the door, his toes barely over the threshold. "S'okay if we come in?"

"Of course it is, sweetheart. Is Rick with you?"

"No, it's me." An older woman with graying hair curled to perfection stepped in behind Joey. Of medium height and build, she wore a deep-red pantsuit which looked expensive enough to have been bought at one of the upscale department stores Kate couldn't afford. "I'm Alice McNeal."

Kate froze. Rick's mother. What must she think of Kate, who was stealing all her son's money and spare time? "Mrs. McNeal. It's good to finally meet you. I have to thank you for taking care of Joey all this—"

"Please call me Alice, dear. Mrs. McNeal sounds so formal." Alice smiled as she helped Joey out of his light jacket. "As for taking care of this dear boy, rest assured it has not been a chore. I've enjoyed every minute of it."

"That's what Rick keeps saying." Kate tried not to frown. "He's told me a lot about you."

"I'm sure he has." She smiled like a proud mother. "And Joey's told me all about you."

Kate glanced at the side of her bed to see her son's blue eyes barely peeking over the high mattress. "And just what have you told Mrs. McNeal?"

"Huh?"

"He calls me Miss Alice."

Kate nodded. "What have you told Miss Alice?"

Joey scrunched his face in thought. "Well, I tolded her about my school in Jackson, and about Bert on Sesame Street, and 'member Snickers?" He glanced up at Alice. "He was my cat who got runned over."

"Yes, you told me about Snickers." Alice beamed at Joey.

Like a proud grandmother, Kate thought. "Sounds as if everything you told her was about you, not me."

"He told me how you read to him, and the games you play and about the time you spend together."

Joey nodded. "Yeah."

"That's a lot." Kate smiled at her son. "Can I have a hug?"

Joey's face brightened. "Sure, Mommy."

"I can't help you up on the bed. Can you climb up all by yourself?"

Joey climbed up and over the rail with help from Alice.

"Be careful, Joey," Alice said. "Your mother's still hurt. Sit on this side of her. Looks like that's her good side."

Joey was all carefulness as he knelt on Kate's right side. She wrapped her good arm around him and hugged him tight. "I've missed you, baby. What's this you're wearing? Another new outfit?"

Joey's dark-blue khakis were a designer name. Definitely not the brand she usually bought him at Wal-Mart. His yellow polo-style shirt had an alligator on the chest.

Joey rubbed his hands down the shirt. "Uh-huh."

Kate couldn't stop her frown. "I don't think I've seen you in the same shirt twice."

"Oh, I know what you're going to say." Alice tried to appear sheepish, but couldn't quite make the look work. "And Rick told me a week ago to stop shopping for Joey, but it's been such a long time since I've had a little one to buy for. I'm having so much fun."

"Where are his clothes?"

Alice's brows lifted in confusion. "Oh, my dear…don't you know?"

Kate's heart dropped several floors. A look like that definitely couldn't be good news. "Know what?"

"All of your things were lost."

"Lost?" Her heart disappeared altogether. "How? When?"

"The police had your car towed while Rick was here at the hospital with you. By the time he thought about asking for it—which was about the time you came to, I think—they'd destroyed it."

"Destroyed it? Who?"

"I don't know. The place where they towed it. A junkyard, I assume."

"Mommy?"

Kate ruffled Joey's hair as she tried to control the panic racing through her. "It's okay, baby. Everything's going to be okay."

But it wasn't. She knew she didn't have a job or an apartment, but no clothes, no dishes, no sheets, no bed? She and Joey were truly homeless.

Her worst nightmare.

She had a few hundred dollars in the bank, but not enough for a wardrobe. Not even enough to get her through a week at a new job. She would have to borrow money. But what bank would give her a loan now?

"Of course everything's going to be all right," Alice said with a pat on Joey's back. "Rick will see to that."

Kate swallowed hard. Her second worst nightmare. "I just... How am I ever going to repay you for taking care of Joey? And for buying these clothes?"

She felt as if she was being smothered under an avalanche of debt.

Alice patted her arm. "Don't you worry about that, dear. Not for a single minute. Having a young man around the house is more than enough payment for me. We have a lot of fun, don't we, Joey?"

"Oh, yes!" Joey turned excited eyes to Kate. "We went to a mooseum for kids and they let me touch all the stuff and play with it and they had movies and toys and ever'thing!"

Kate smoothed his shirt and tried to smile. She had never let Joey know how desperate their situation was. Then again, it had never been this desperate. "I'm glad you're having a good time. But save something in Memphis to do with me, okay?"

"I will, Mommy." Joey leaned forward and kissed her cheek.

They talked for a while, mostly Joey telling her what he and Alice did to fill their days together and what he and Rick did in the evenings.

"Are you ready, Joey?" Alice asked twenty minutes later.

"Do you have to go so soon?" Kate asked.

"Yes, I'm sorry. I have a contractor coming over in half an hour. I'm having my two spare bedrooms converted into a master suite."

Joey started to get up, but Kate held on to his shirt. "You going to give me another kiss before you leave?"

Joey gave her a noisy smack on her cheek and a wonderfully warm bear hug. "Bye, Mommy. I see you later. Rick said he'd bring me, too."

"Good. I can never have too many Joey hugs."

Alice held out her arms to help him down. Then she smiled at Kate. "I'll bring him back tomorrow. Can I get you anything? I know how dreary and sparse hospital rooms can be. Though this one isn't too bad."

How about a new wardrobe? "I'm fine. I should be leaving the hospital tomorrow or the next day."

"You sure?"

Kate hesitated. She hated asking for anything. "Well…"

"Yes?" Alice perked up, her eyes sparkling.

"Could I…" Kate tried to breathe. Why was it so hard to breathe? "Could I possibly…"

"Yes, dear?"

"Could I borrow a dress or some pants or something? I don't have anything to wear when I leave the hospital."

"Goodness sake, child!" Alice laughed out loud. "My clothes would swallow you whole. I'll buy you something."

"No! Please don't—"

"What size do you wear?" She squinted at Kate's figure. "You're about an eight, I'd guess, right? And a small in lingerie?"

"Well, yes. Okay, but a sweatshirt and pants from Wal-Mart would—"

"Don't worry, dear. I'll take care of everything!" She pushed Joey toward the door. "We'll see you later."

"Alice, please—"

"You take care, dear. Bye!"

With that, they were gone.

Kate stared at the door in shock, then leaned back against the pillow with a huff. She could certainly see where Rick got his stubbornness. What part of *no* did the McNeals not understand?

Chapter Five

Rick stepped off the elevator and stopped short.

Kate was making her way slowly down the hall on crutches. Her left leg was still bound in a brace from her thigh to her ankle. She held it off the floor as she took step after painstaking step.

His first reaction hit him like a sledgehammer in his chest—pure, unadulterated lust.

She was wearing the nightgown and robe that he'd commissioned his mother to buy so Kate would have something besides the open-backed gowns the hospital provided. Not until now did Rick realize how diabolical his mother was.

Instead of the warm, practical, totally unrevealing flannel set he'd envisioned, Alice had purchased a lacy, satiny set that floated around Kate's curves with every move. Neither gown nor robe was transparent. Still, for what Rick couldn't see, his libido supplied a detailed, vivid image.

Rick was a sucker for romantic, tantalizing lingerie. Thanks to the close relationship between Stacy and his mother, Alice knew it. He just never thought his own mother would use her intimate knowledge against him.

What was she thinking?

The trouble was, Rick knew what Alice was thinking. She was thinking exactly what she'd been saying for the past year and a half—that it was high time he got past the fact that he'd lost Stacy and move on with his life. He wanted children and she wanted grandchildren. In order to accomplish both their goals, he needed a wife.

He closed his eyes and snapped the lid tightly over his libido. What was *he* thinking? This was a hospital, for God's sake, not a candlelit dinner for two. Kate had been lying in a coma just five days ago. Now she had a broken arm and leg, plus a punk hair-do because of eighteen stitches in her head.

He needed stitches in *his* head. This was not the time or place—or woman, for that matter—for sexual fantasies. He was helping Kate get back on her feet, literally. That was the extent of their relationship.

Reining in his thoughts took a moment, because he hadn't had to exercise this kind of control in a long, long time.

When he was finally able to open his eyes and watch Kate more objectively, it was Rick's heart that responded, not his libido. He saw a woman who needed help. His help. He wanted to run to her, pick her up and carry her where she needed to go.

But he knew she wasn't going anywhere in particular, just practicing with the crutches. He also knew carrying her was the last thing she would allow.

Stubborn woman.

She spotted him then and stopped, her emotions clear on her face.

First he saw surprise, then sheepishness because he'd caught her; then, as if to prove his point, she lifted her chin.

Rick covered the distance between them. "I suppose tomorrow you'll be running in the 10K for St. Jude."

She sniffed and turned to head in the opposite direction, saying over her shoulder, "I have to build up my strength."

"It's more likely you'll hurt yourself, doing too much too soon. Did the doctor okay this?"

"He told me to walk when I felt like walking. These crutches were delivered to my room an hour ago, so I decided to—" Her words were cut off as she stumbled.

Rick caught her before she fell against the hard wall. The crutches crashed to the floor. He lifted her easily. As her warm weight settled in his arms and her arms wrapped around his neck, desire flashed through him again.

Then he looked down at her pinched face, and the fire inside him died as quickly as it had flared. "What happened?"

"I don't know." She took quick, shallow breaths. "The right crutch suddenly shot out from under my arm."

He didn't say "I told you so," just carried her back to her room.

"My crutches…"

"I'll get them in a minute."

"Someone will take them and, seeing as they came from the hospital, they probably cost four hundred dollars."

Rick pushed open the door to her room with his foot. "If they need the crutches that badly, let them have them. We can always get you another pair."

"Easy for you to— Oh!" She cried out as he laid her on the bed.

He froze with his arm still under her knees. "Did I hurt you?"

Her teeth had a firm grip on her bottom lip as she shook her head. "I'm okay."

He sighed in disgust. "You'd say that if you were bleeding to death, wouldn't you?"

He didn't expect an answer and didn't get one. He gave her a moment to recover by retrieving the crutches which still lay where they'd left them. As he picked up the right one, it slid apart.

Shaking his head, he returned to her room and held the pieces over the end of the bed. "Who adjusted these?"

"Oh. I guess I didn't tighten them enough."

"Someone didn't show you how to use them?" He spun for the door. "I'm going to let someone have an earful of—"

"No!"

He stopped and turned back to her. "A therapist should've adjusted them, then given you instructions. The hospital has a liability here—"

"It's my fault." Her gaze dropped to the end of the bed. "The man who brought them said a therapist would be in after supper."

He should've known. "You just couldn't wait, could you?"

Her voice was small as she said, "No."

"Kate…"

"Where's Joey? I thought you were bringing him with you tonight."

Shaking his head, Rick let her change the subject. He set one crutch down on the end of the bed so he could adjust and tighten the other. "Mom imported a boy his age to play this afternoon. Mike Garner from the church. They were having such a good time when I called, I decided to let them play. I'll bring him after supper."

Rick didn't notice Kate's silence until he'd tightened both crutches and leaned them against the wall. He turned to see the fingers of her good hand picking nervously at the sheet.

"What's wrong now?"

She glanced up, then back down. "Dr. Lowry said he'll probably release me tomorrow."

"And that's not a good thing? I know Joey will be jumping for joy to have you home. Though I think Mom should take care of him for a few more days, at least. Oh, I didn't tell you about that, did I? As it turns out—"

"Why are you doing this, Rick? I'm practically a stranger to you and your mother. You've paid my hospital bill. You don't owe me anything else now that I'm okay."

"But you're not okay. This crutch incident proves that. You're not strong enough to be on your own. And where would you go if you were? You don't even have a car to live out of."

"Why, Rick? *Why?*"

He stepped closer to the bed. "Because you need me, Kate. And I—"

I need you.

Those were the words he'd stopped himself from uttering.

But they weren't true... Were they? No. He didn't need Kate. He liked her, and he liked helping her, but he didn't need her.

"You what?" she prompted.

Rick hesitated. He couldn't tell her why he was being so insistent, because he didn't know.

He lifted a helpless hand. "Because Mother needs something to occupy her, and she's become attached to Joey. Because I... Hell, I just have to, that's all. I can't explain it because I don't understand it myself. All I know is that you need help, and there's no way I can let you just walk away. I have to help you get back on your feet. I do owe it to you, Kate. And I owe it to Joey. *You* owe it to Joey to let me."

Kate frowned at the foot of the bed for a long moment. Finally she said, "All right. For Joey."

"Thank you."

"Did you call about my job? And my apartment? What's happening with the insurance?"

He nodded grimly. "You were right about your job. Someone's already started the one you were hired for."

"Did you tell Mr. Rayburn what happened?"

"Yes. He said he was sorry, but he didn't have anything else to offer you at the moment. He said you can check back when you're up to it."

"I see."

"Your apartment's gone, too."

"Along with all of our clothes and—" She cut herself off. "No need to dwell on all that. The insurance?"

He shrugged. "The Cadillac driver is contesting everything, saying I shouldn't have been in the middle of the road—which is right. Saying the hill is the same thing as a blind curve, which makes the rear-ending law iffy. It may go to trial, if the lawyers can't settle it. If it does, it will probably be a few months."

"So I can't get a new car until then."

"I can loan you—"

"No."

"I bought myself a new—"

"No, Rick. I can't take any more of your money." She heaved a defeated sigh. "But that makes you right, doesn't it? Joey and I won't even have a car to live out of. I guess we'll have to stay with your mother, then, if she'll have us. But just until my casts are removed."

"About my mother's…"

"What?"

"It seems she's having some work done on her house." He held his hands up defensively. "I didn't know about it. Honest."

"She did mention an appointment with a contractor today."

"You won't be able to stay there. She's having a wall removed in the guest bedroom. God only knows what bee landed in her bonnet, but it's going to be a mess."

"Then…"

He met her eyes squarely. "You'll have to come to my house."

He waited for the explosion.

Surprisingly, Kate answered calmly, though there was a dead quality to the calm. "You live in a condominium. Do you have enough room for both me and Joey?"

Rick nodded. "It's three bedrooms. I don't have a bed in the room I use as an office, but I'll bring one over from Mom's."

She seemed surprised by his answer.

"What?" he asked. "Did you expect me to say you had to sleep with Joey?"

She shook her head. "I wouldn't mind that."

"Then what? On the couch? The floor?" Then it dawned on him. His eyes narrowed. "You expected me to say you had to sleep with me."

The thought was so provocative, his libido flared again. And it wasn't all sexual. To have someone warm and soft in his bed again, someone to reach for in the cold hours of the night, was as seductive as sinking into her willing, wanting body.

He quickly tamped the desire down and noticed her gaze had slid away.

He cursed under his breath. "What have I ever done to make you think I would do something like that?"

Her chin lifted. "I learned young—real young—that when someone gives you something or does something for you, they want something in return."

He stiffened with rage. "You mean you had to—"

"No," she said hastily. "I never did that. But I don't have anything else with which to repay you, do I?"

He studied her defiant, stubborn face. What had she gone through? How had she been raised, to have such an opinion about people?

Another kind of desire gripped him then. He wanted to know exactly how she'd lived, up until now. In fact, he wanted to know everything about her. He'd never met anyone like her. She was so strong, so independent, so breathtakingly beautiful, even lying in a hospital bed.

Nothing else to give? Kate Burnett had everything to give to some lucky man.

Rick shifted on his feet.

But not him. He wasn't lucky, and he wasn't looking for a wife at this point in his life—no matter what his mother said. He probably never would. He'd had Stacy. Lovely, sweet, mild-mannered Stacy. The love of his life. The *only* love of his life. Although…

He couldn't remember the exact shade of her hair.

"Look, Rick. I'm going to let you off the hook. You've made the offer. I thank you very much for taking care of me, and taking care of Joey. But you don't have to—"

"Forget it, Kate." Rick shook off his fading memories. "You've already agreed to stay with me. You're not getting out of it."

"But what do you get out of it?"

He could give her some fancy sentiments about the true meaning of charity, but she deserved the truth…even though the truth wasn't easy for him to admit. "I get a house that isn't empty for another few weeks."

She blinked in surprise.

He went on. "I can't tell you how much I've enjoyed having Joey around. Instead of you thanking me for taking care of him, I should be thanking you for letting me."

She studied his face. "You sound as if you're lonely."

"I guess…" He didn't realize it would be so hard to admit. "I have been."

"But wh—"

"Let's get back to the original subject, shall we?" He certainly didn't want a full-fledged soul baring at the moment, and Kate didn't need the pressure.

She looked as if she wanted to argue, but after a moment she gave in. "What was the original subject?"

He smiled. "I think we were discussing sleeping arrangements. I said I needed to bring a bed over from Mom's. No doubt, if you hadn't become side-tracked, you would have told me I shouldn't go to the trouble."

"Well, you shouldn't. Not for me. I can sleep on anything."

"Well, that may be true, but Mom informed me this morning that I have to store some of her furniture, with all the construction going on. It's just as easy to bring it to my place as to a storage facility." When she didn't protest further, he felt kinks he didn't know were in his shoulders relax. "You can have the guest room. I'll put a single bed in the other guest bedroom—which I use as an office—for Joey. He'll love being in the same room as the computer. He's really taking to it, you know. Like a duck to water."

"They had a computer at the day care where he stayed in Jackson, and he was always talking about it. I was saving money to buy him one for Christmas." She took a ragged breath. "Now I'll have to use that money to start our lives over again."

Rick stepped up beside the bed. He hated seeing Kate so concerned. He wanted to kiss the wrinkles from her forehead, but he settled for taking her cold hand in his. "Don't worry, beau—Kate. I replace perfectly usable computers all the time, just to keep my employees happy with bigger, better, faster. When you find your own place, Joey can have one of the old ones."

"Oh, we couldn't—"

"Yes, you can. I can't sell them because everyone wants the newest RAM-eating monster available. We give them away—high schools, community centers. Whoever wants them. At least with Joey, I know it will have a loving home."

In spite of his joke, his words depressed him. When she and Joey left, he'd be faced with the empty, echoing rooms of his house again.

Dark, hollow, lonely. Like his soul had been for three long years.

Nearing midnight, a sleepless Kate sat on the side of the hospital bed, staring in wonder at the ensemble draped across her lap. Though a tad pretentious, *ensemble* was the only word that fit. She certainly couldn't call such elegance merely a dress or even an outfit.

Alice had sent the promised clothes via Rick and Joey when they'd come back to the hospital around seven.

The navy-blue dress was fashioned from the finest, thinnest, softest wool Kate had ever rubbed her hands across. Long enough to cover most of her cast yet short enough not to trip her, the skirt floated around her legs like a dark cloud. A wide belt covered with the same wool defined her waist.

Flat leather shoes matched the navy dress perfectly, a feat of shopping in itself. The straps across the instep would keep the shoes on, so Kate wouldn't walk out of them, though she'd only be wearing one.

A black blazer, made of much heavier wool, would keep her warm. But the best part...

Kate fingered delicate silk.

The best part was the lingerie—bra and panties of black silk and lace, plus a matching half slip.

Tears stung her eyes. She'd never possessed anything so fine. As a child, she and her mother would shop at second-hand stores or would take clothes from whichever charity was giving them away at the time. As an adult, she'd vowed never to wear hand-me-downs again. But all she could afford new was the sale rack at Wal-Mart—when she could afford anything at all. Most of the clothing budget was spent on Joey, who seemed to grow an inch a month.

Kate had been appalled at the expensive clothes, calling Alice to insist she return them and buy her some cheap sweats. Alice had seemed genuinely confused, even a little hurt. She'd explained that pants wouldn't be practical, with the cast on her leg.

When Kate said she'd seen an ad in the Sunday paper advertising velveteen dresses at Target for under twenty dollars, Alice had countered with a soft but chiding lecture on how much warmer wool was than cheap velveteen. The classic lines would be fashionable forever and if taken care of, this dress would last long enough for Kate to be buried in it.

The only reason Kate had given in was because Alice acted hurt that Kate wouldn't give her the pleasure of buying for a young woman again.

Kate had done a lot of giving in since the McNeals had entered their lives. She justified her weakness by telling herself that she had no choice but to accept their help, that she had to think of Joey.

But her acquiescence alarmed her. This wasn't who she was. Ever since she'd been old enough to support herself, she'd refused to accept charity from anyone, even close friends.

What was wrong with her? Did she have more brain damage than Dr. Lowry thought?

With a sigh Kate rubbed her temples. Her head hurt from worrying.

She adjusted the bed so she could stretch out. After she'd settled under the covers and was just about to turn off the light, the wool dress caught her eye. Reaching down, she pulled it across her, feeling the added warmth immediately.

She brought one of the sleeves up to her nose so she could breathe the earthy scent. With a sleepy sigh, she nuzzled the soft wool against her cheek and let dreams overtake her.

"It's that one, Mommy," Joey called from the back seat. "There."

Rick eased slowly over the flat speed bump. Kate hadn't said a word since they'd entered the upscale condominiums. But then, she hadn't said much since they'd left the hospital.

"Where?" She turned to see where Joey was pointing, but stopped herself at half a turn. "I'm sorry, baby. I can't tell which way you're pointing."

Rick couldn't tell whether her frown came from pain at the motion or the fact that they were almost at his house.

"It's the last one on the left." Rick turned on his left blinker even though there were no vehicles on the narrow street lined with two-and-a-half-story brick town homes. "The one with green shutters."

He watched her out the corner of his eye, but couldn't

tell what she thought about his house. Not that it mattered. She was only staying here a few weeks.

He pressed the garage-door opener on his visor, then turned carefully into the two-car garage comprising half the front of his house.

Kate eyed the pegboard hanging on the wall behind a long workbench on the side closest to her. "Do you always keep everything so organized? I've never seen a garage so…neat."

Rick frowned as he switched off the ignition and followed her gaze.

Every tool hung in precise order in descending size from left to right, each neatly outlined so an idiot could tell where each tool should be replaced. He'd spent the first six months after Stacy died on the project, mostly in the wee hours of the morning. It had given him something to do, something to occupy his hands and mind, something to keep him from taking the hedge clippers to his throat.

Now, however, he saw the wall as she saw it—evidence of a nasty streak of obsessive-compulsive behavior.

"Not always," he admitted. "Just in the past three years."

She glanced at him sharply.

"Stacy was always after me to straighten my tools." He shrugged. "I finally did."

"Who's Stacy?"

Rick twisted to find Joey unfastening the straps on his car seat. "She was a lady I knew a long time ago."

Joey finally freed himself from the straps. "Mommy, I'll get your crutches, 'kay?"

"What?" Kate shook her head and blinked, as if she had to bring herself back from a place far away. "Okay, Joey. Thank you."

"You help your mom a lot, don't you, Joey?"

The boy's head was bent between the front and back seats, reaching for the crutches laid between them. "Yes, sir. Mommy needs me. I need her."

It sounded like a family mantra, and Joey proceeded to prove it during the half hour it took to get Kate settled in the guest room that Rick had helped the boy vacate the night before. Instead of running off to watch television or play his computer games, Joey helped Rick carry Kate's few things into the house, then hovered solicitously on the stairs as his mother ascended with excruciating slowness to the second floor.

Rick did some hovering himself. He wanted to pick her up half a dozen times and carry her up the carpeted stairs, but the first time he suggested it, Kate backed him down two steps with a "touch me and you die" glint in her eyes. When he offered to carry the single bed downstairs to the mostly unused dining room, she halted him in midsentence with the same mulish look.

Finally, she stretched out on the firm queen-size bed in the guest room. Her face was pinched and white, showing how much moving had cost her.

"Can I get you anything?" he asked. "Water? A cold drink? A fifth of whisky?"

She tried to smile at his weak joke but wasn't successful. She shook her head. "I'm fine."

Rick studied her lovely, waxen face as she closed her eyes. She hadn't complained a single time of pain, hadn't mentioned any discomfort whatsoever. But she obviously was weak and hurting.

He wished he could take it all away—onto himself, if need be. She was too frail to have to be this strong.

Just as he noticed Joey was no longer in the room, the boy entered slowly, balancing a tray with a sandwich, a cup of prepackaged applesauce and an unopened cold drink. "Look, Mommy. I made you lunch."

Rick backed out of Joey's way.

"Thank you, baby." Kate beamed weakly at her son. "Just lay it here beside me for now, okay?"

Joey placed the tray on the bed beside her, then stepped back and waited. When Kate made no move to touch the food, the boy said, "You don't like p'nut butter samiches anymore?"

"Of course I do. They're my favorite. I just—" she shivered "—I just need to catch my breath is all."

"I think he's trying to tell you that you need to eat," Rick said. "Even a four-year-old knows you need to build up your strength."

Kate frowned at him, but instead of refusing, she picked up the soft drink and pulled at the tab…and pulled and pulled.

Rick's heart turned over. She was too weak to even open a can.

He stepped forward, reaching for the drink. "Let me help you."

She held the can away from him. "I can do it."

Pain made her voice sharp. Pain or stubbornness. Which was it?

She set the drink back on the tray. "Please, I need to rest."

He nodded, refusing to be hurt by her rebuff. He knew what pain can do to anyone—and it didn't have to be physical.

"All right then. We'll leave you alone." He turned. "Come on, Joey."

Rick paused at the door in time to see Joey step closer to the bed and push the tray another inch toward his mother.

"Please eat, Mommy. Alice says good foods makes you big and strong."

Kate smiled at her son, her eyes filled with love. "All right."

She picked up the sandwich and began to eat. Just a nibble, true, but nibbles added up.

Rick noticed a dab of peanut butter on the side of Kate's mouth a second before her pointed tongue swiped it away.

Desire swept through him, so strong it grabbed his feet and nailed them to the floor.

"See ya later, Mommy." Joey took Rick's hand. "Time for *Star Trek*."

"Huh? Oh yeah." He'd introduced Joey to reruns of the original series.

"You going to be all right, Kate?" Rick asked from the doorway.

"Yes." She glanced away, then back at him with resolution. "Thank you, Rick, for all you've done."

"My pleasure," he murmured, then allowed Joey to pull him from the room.

As he sat beside Joey, blindly watching television, Rick contemplated the desire he felt for her. He hadn't reacted sexually to a woman in years.

But mixed in with desire for Kate was the need to be part of such a loving, sharing family. A family who needed each other. He wanted Kate to turn to him, to let him help her, to *ask* him to help her. It had been so long since anyone had been that close to him, so long since anyone had needed him enough to ask.

But he knew it was going to be even longer.

Kate accepted Joey's help, but wouldn't let Rick get her a glass of water. He tried to deny that the twinge in his chest was jealousy, but he couldn't lie to himself. Rick wanted her to ask *him*.

Was it because she loved Joey that she could accept his help? Or was it another lesson intended to strengthen the boy's independence?

Whether love or lessons motivated her didn't matter. She obviously was not the woman for him, no matter how much desire he felt for her. He needed someone who needed him.

Kate might need him now, but she hated that fact. She would leave his house—leave him—as soon as she was strong enough to walk out the door.

Rick knew this as certainly as he knew Spock's ears were pointed.

Now all he had to do was convince his libido.

Chapter Six

Kate woke abruptly the next morning, disoriented.

Where was she? How did she get here? Where was Joey?

As she struggled to sit up, the faintest trace of a scent caught her attention. Rick. She was at Rick's house.

Relieved, she relaxed against the pillow where her smile slowly flattened.

She knew what she'd recognized—the scent of his aftershave. She had no idea what he used—something earthy, woodsy, not at all flowery or sweet. She liked it. Still...

Why had she known it immediately? Her subconscious connected it with Rick before her brain could register a scent. And above all, why did recognizing it make her relax?

To escape the unanswerable questions and the growing intimacy they implied, she turned her head only to blink at the sunlight streaming through the curtains.

What time was it? Where was everyone? Had Rick taken Joey to Alice's and gone to work, leaving her alone?

Kate succeeded in sitting up this time and was pushing

back the covers when a faint but reassuring sound drifted in through the space left by the slightly opened door.

"Joey!" Rick said in a muted tone. "We weren't going to wake her up, remember?"

"I'm quiet as an itty-bitty mouse, Rick." Joey told him in the same stage whisper. "I jus' wanna peek and—"

"I'm awake, baby," Kate called. "Come on in."

Immediate clomping made her smile. Seconds later Joey shoved open the door. "Mommy! You finally woke up."

She held out her right arm, and he rushed over for a hug.

"Why are you—" Rick stood in the open door, hands on hips, watching her intently, his brown eyes warmer than she'd ever seen them "—up?"

Kate's heart skipped a beat, then she remembered that all she had on was the satin nightgown Alice had bought for her. And her struggles to sit up had twisted it around her thighs.

Feeling heat sting her cheeks, she pulled the sheet across the front of her body and bent over Joey, helping him climb onto the bed next to her.

What troubled her more than Rick's look was the way she'd responded. Like a teenager getting all excited when a cute boy said hello.

But that couldn't be right. She was no inexperienced kid. She was a mother, for Pete's sake.

Her heart had simply reacted to being caught—although at what she didn't know. She had every right to sit up if she wanted. But her pulse *hadn't* gone haywire at the sight of his ruggedly handsome face.

Ruggedly? Where had that come from? The word implied she had some opinion on his face, that she'd been giving it some thought—and she hadn't. She didn't.

Joey drew all her attention then, as he knelt on the mattress and hugged her. "I thought you was never gonna wake up, Mommy."

With relief, she lost herself in the hug, holding her son's

small warm body tight against her. They'd come so close to never being able to hug again.

"Not too tight, Joey," Rick said.

"He's not hurting me," she protested, barely keeping the frown off her face when Joey released her, anyway.

Troubled that Joey had responded to Rick's command rather than her implied invitation, Kate looked around for a clock. "What time is it?"

"It's almost ten." Rick stepped closer. "Are you hungry?"

"Ten? I can't believe I slept so long. I went to sleep at eight, didn't I?"

"Seven forty-five. You're still weak. It's no wonder."

She craned her neck back so she could see his face. "I am a bit hungry. But I don't want you to go to any trouble."

"With this kid?" Rick smiled. "He's had a bowl of cereal waiting for you since six."

"Cheerios," Joey announced.

"Mmm. My favorite." Kate reached for the crutches leaning against the chest of drawers. "I'll be down in a minute."

Rick caught them first and held them away. "Why don't I carry you down? It's faster and much safer."

Kate shivered as she thought about the day before, when he'd insisted on carrying her down the stairs and then back up to bed. Even though she knew he was only doing it to be nice, somehow it had seemed unbearably intimate. "That's okay."

"You're still not strong enough to negotiate them by—"

"I can do it myself."

With a disgusted huff, Rick turned to Joey. "Tell me, little guy. Does your mother ever use the word yes?"

Joey looked confused. "Yeah."

"I need to freshen up first," Kate insisted. "Unless you're going to carry me into the bathroom for a tooth brushing and sponge bath, you—"

"I can do that."

Unable to believe her ears, she glanced up to see his sexy grin. She was so surprised—was he actually flirting with her?—that she couldn't stop a nervous laugh. "Sure. I'm going to let you do *that*."

"Hey. You can't blame a guy for trying."

Yes, she could, and she usually did. But at the moment, Kate felt flattered, excited. Which wasn't good. Not good at all.

"Trying what, Rick?" Joey asked brightly.

Chuckling, Rick mussed Joey's hair. "One day you'll understand."

Kate swallowed her embarrassment and held out her hands expectantly. "Crutches, please. I have to build up my strength or I'll never get back to work."

"But you—"

"Either give them to me or I won't come downstairs until I get this stupid cast off my leg."

"We can serve her breakfast in bed, can't we, little guy?"

"Sure, Rick." Joey jumped off the bed. "I'll go—"

"Wait a minute," she called. With narrowed eyes she glanced up at Rick. Why did the man have to be so tall? And so darned accommodating? "I can't stand the thought of another day in bed."

"Then—"

"You haven't even let me attempt to go down the stairs by myself. At least let me try."

He studied her face for a moment, then sighed. "We'll see how you do."

Feeling as if he'd just given her a dozen roses, she let him ease her to her feet. He started to position the crutches under her arms, but grabbed the matching robe off the bed instead.

"Here, put this on," he said hoarsely. "It's...a little chilly today."

Blushing again, she put on the robe, tied the slippery belt

as best she could, then accepted the crutches. She was a little sore under her arms from walking with them yesterday, but she also was determined to be as little a burden as possible, which meant getting around on her own.

One look in the bathroom mirror made her certain she'd imagined Rick flirting with her. Who could be attracted to a woman with an angry red scar crawling back into a ghastly mess of hair? The bruises were mostly gone, but her eyes were red and swollen.

With a sigh, Kate completed her limited ablutions. She would've liked a hot shower or bath, but they were forbidden to her until the casts came off.

She came out of the bathroom five minutes later and walked to the top of the stairs. And swallowed.

They were awfully high.

She stood at the top several minutes, trying to figure out a way to descend safely. Funny, they hadn't seemed quite as steep when Rick carried her down last night.

Finally she had to admit she couldn't get down them on her own. Attempting it was downright stupid. She had a son to care for, a job to find. One slip and she'd be off work even longer, if not permanently.

Tears stung her eyes. She had to ask Rick for help, which was tantamount to admitting she couldn't take care of herself.

Why did this have to happen to her? She hated being helpless, hated being at the mercy of strangers.

Before a tear could fall, Rick appeared at the bottom of the stairs. He locked gazes with her a moment, then climbed up. He took her crutches from her, leaned them against the wall, then lifted her easily into his arms. Never saying a word, he carried her down and set her on her feet at the bottom.

Joey ran up the stairs and retrieved her crutches.

Kate took them from her son, one by one.

"I'll get acupa coffee for ya, Mommy!" He ran toward the kitchen.

"Thank you," Rick said.

Surprised, Kate finally looked at him. "That's supposed to be my line, isn't it?"

He lifted a shoulder. "You can use it, too."

She settled the crutches under her arms. "Why are you thanking me?"

He stepped back against the wall, leaving her room to pass down the hall. "For not trying to get down the stairs on your own."

His quiet understanding made her feel even worse. Humbled, feeling like a shrew, Kate started toward the kitchen. "I realized I could be injured all over again. I may be stubborn, but I'm not stupid."

To his credit, he didn't agree with her.

A few steps from the kitchen, she stopped and half turned. "Thank you, Rick, for helping me and—" she took a deep breath "—for not making me ask."

His face relaxed into a beautiful smile. "You're welcome."

Fifteen minutes later Kate swallowed her last bite of Cheerios when the dateline of the Memphis newspaper registered. "It's Wednesday."

Rick glanced up from the comics Joey was reading to him. "All day."

"Shouldn't you be at work?"

"I would be on a normal day, yes. But I took off to take care of y—"

"No!" Kate was horrified. "You can't do that."

"Of course I can. I own the company. Besides, I haven't had a vacation in over three ye—"

"You're wasting your vacation taking care of me?" This was getting worse by the minute.

"I wouldn't call it wasting—"

"Go to work. Now. Please. You've missed nearly half a day already."

Rick was clearly confused by her insistence. "Why?"

Kate's concern for the future merged with her frustration over her helplessness into something close to panic.

By the look on his face, Rick sensed it.

She disguised a deep, calming breath by taking a too-large gulp of coffee. She had to seem reasonable. She had to seem *capable,* or he would never go. "I don't want to cost you any more money. Please go to work, Rick. I'm downstairs now. Joey and I will be fine."

"Oh, no. There's no telling what you'll try to do if I'm not here. Probably try to swim fifty laps in the pool."

She managed a smile at his joke. "I promise I won't do anything stupid. If I need something, Joey can help me."

Rick considered her statement, then shook his head. "Joey can get into as much trouble as you. He makes coffee, for God's sake. What's he going to try next? Grilling a steak? No, it's better if I stay here."

"Joey wouldn't do anything like that, would you, Joey?"

Joey's shoulders came up to his ears. "I don't know how."

Kate frowned at her son's implication that he would if he did know how. "He wouldn't. I've always taught him to be careful."

"I know you have, and you've taught him well. He's an amazing kid. But he's a kid, and I think sometimes you ask too much of him. Taking care of you right now is a job for a grown-up. Let me help you, Kate, at least until you're strong enough to do things on your own. All you have to do is ask."

He made it sound so easy. Just ask.

She studied his strong face, clean-shaven, even though he didn't plan on going to work. He seemed sincere, but she'd been fooled before. People extending charity say they don't expect anything from you, but they always do.

"You've done so much already." She tried to keep the overtones of accusation from her voice, but wasn't entirely successful. She couldn't help but think about all he'd done, and all he was going to do...and what he wanted in return.

Whatever he wanted from her, she couldn't let him add keeping him from work to the list of things she owed him. "We've taken up so much of your time. You must've missed a lot of work when I was in the hospital. I'll be fine. I promise."

"Kate…"

Why was he being so stubborn? "Please go to work, Rick. We don't need you."

He froze.

Kate froze, too, at the hurt she saw on his face. She knew exactly what she'd done. All he wanted was for her to admit she needed his help—just a little—and she'd thrown his need to be needed back in his face.

She'd be surprised if he didn't throw her out of his house.

But he didn't. He merely rose from the table and walked out.

Kate had to cover her mouth to keep from calling him back.

"Mommy? You okay?"

No, she wasn't okay. At the moment she hated herself— for what she'd said, for the way she'd said it, for being so much trouble.

But most of all she hated having Rick think of her as helpless, as someone who needed charity, as just some burden to be lifted and toted here and there. She, who was so independent, so capable of taking care of herself.

What had she done to him? Was he coming back?

Kate swallowed her fear and smiled at Joey. "Sure, baby. I'm fine. Everything's going to be…"

She couldn't finish.

Rick gunned his car to life, but by the time the garage door had lifted, his anger was as cool as the mid-March air.

What had just happened? What had sent Kate off into such a snit for him to leave? The thought of him missing a few days' pay? He'd told her he owned the company. Hell, he made so much money and spent so little, he could sell Data Enterprises and stay home for the rest of his life.

But Kate didn't know that. All she saw was the money *she* wasn't making by being off work, and equated that to him.

He had to remember she was still hurting, still not operating at 100 percent capacity. She hated not being able to take care of herself, and he couldn't blame her. If he were honest with himself, he had to admit he would hate it, too.

In fact, if he were honest with himself, he had to admit a lot of things. The first and foremost was the fact that he was attracted to Kate, in a way that he'd never been attracted to any woman. Before she even woke from the coma, he'd admired her for raising such a fine son. When she finally had come out of the coma, he liked her grit and determination. Now…

The memory of how sexy she was with the nightgown twisted around her thighs made him have to fight a very obvious physiological reaction even now. There was no getting away from the fact that he was attracted to her physically. Even in her condition.

Geez, he felt like such a sleazeball. She couldn't even walk, for God's sake. She was still hurting, still battered, still bruised. And if he wanted her now, what was going to happen when she was well and whole and even more beautiful?

Damn.

Had she sensed his desire? Was that why she'd panicked?

Yes and no. She'd blushed and covered herself when she'd noticed his lust-inspired stupefaction—but shyly, not with fear or anger.

Could she be attracted to him, too? Was it possible?

The idea made desire flare all over again. Rick mentally stomped the flames.

He couldn't go there—for too many reasons.

He'd assured her adamantly, even angrily, that she didn't have to pay him back for helping her—especially not with sex. Yet here he was wanting her. She was living under his roof, under his protection…which meant he had to protect her against himself as well.

Plus, there was Joey. How could Rick have lustful thoughts about a woman whose son was right there in the house?

Then there was his own mother. What would she say about her son having the hots for a woman he barely knew, a woman he was trying to help, not hurt?

Plus…there was something else, wasn't there? Oh yes, Stacy. How could he forget his wife? He'd fallen in love with Stacy the first time he'd set eyes on her in ninth grade. Aside from the usual schoolboy fantasies over busty actresses, Rick had never really desired another woman. Wanting Kate made him seem…unfaithful, somehow.

Everything about it was wrong.

Wasn't it?

Rick felt as confused as a computer asked to find data that wasn't there. The only thing he knew for sure was that Kate couldn't negotiate the stairs. He had to move her downstairs. Hopefully, being able to get around on her own would help her feel a little more independent.

Realizing that his car had headed automatically toward work like one of those old ice wagon horses, Rick made a left turn and went to his mother's. Since he didn't want Alice to confirm his feelings about his degenerate behavior, he didn't share his concerns with her. He merely answered her questions about Kate and Joey, then loaded the other twin bed in his new Jeep. There was no sign of the contractor, but Alice assured him the workers were due anytime as she handed him a bag of clothes to take home.

With a kiss on his mother's cheek, he headed toward his condo. Halfway there, he realized that for the first time in three years, he actually felt good about going home. There was a family there. Okay, not his family. Still, it wasn't an empty shell of a house now. It contained life.

The minute he carried the box spring in the door, he smelled lunch. Kate must be warming up a can of some beefy kind of soup. His first reaction was to march into the kitchen and take over the job, but he didn't. She could certainly lean on the counter long enough to heat soup.

Rick set the box spring against a hallway wall, then headed toward the kitchen to check on things. He swung open the door and his heart stopped.

Joey, not Kate, was warming soup. The boy stood on a chair in front of the stove.

"What are you doing?" Rick asked.

Joey turned. As he did, a towel in his hand swept across the gas flame.

"Joey, my God! Get away from there!"

Two strides took Rick to the stove. He lifted Joey off the chair, then grabbed the end of the dish towel that was burning. As the smoke detector began to scream, he threw the towel into the sink and doused it with water.

Catching his breath, he turned. Joey stood where Rick had set him, his eyes huge and streaming silent tears.

Rick picked him up and hugged him close. "Thank God you're not hurt. You're not, are you?"

Rick held Joey in one arm to examine him. His shirt had a line of black soot up the front, but there were no burns. Thank God.

Joey shook his head and between hiccuping sobs said, "I'm sorry, Rick."

"I know you are, little guy." Turning back to the stove, he used one hand to turn off the burner and slide the pan of soup to a cool one. "What in the world were you—"

"What is it?" Kate's words screamed down the hall. "Joey, what are you doing? Get out of there! Now!"

"He's all right, Kate," Rick called.

The smoke detector quieted, letting him hear Kate clumping rapidly down the hall.

His eyes narrowed as she appeared in the door, her eyes wide with panic. God was the only one to thank. Kate sure hadn't been around.

Her nightgown swirled around her ankles as she stopped. "What happened?"

He made no attempt to soften his harsh tone. "Where the hell were you?"

"In the bathroom, trying to get clean." Her voice was breathless. "Why? What's all this smoke? Joey, are you okay?"

Joey squirmed in his arms, so Rick set him down. The boy ran to his mother and threw his arms around her waist. "Mommy, I'm sorry. I didn't mean to. Honest!"

Kate let go of her right crutch and hugged him tight. Still holding on to him, she looked up at Rick. "What happened?"

Rick pointed at the pan. "Joey was apparently cooking lunch for you."

Her eyes widened further. "Cooking?"

"When I came in, a dish towel he was holding went up in flames."

Kate grabbed Joey by the shoulders. "What were you doing? I've never taught you how to even turn on the stove."

Joey's tears began anew. "I know, but…but…Miz Alice and me make soup all the time. She lets me stir it. An' I wanted—" he hiccuped again "—I wanted to s'prise you."

"Well, you did, but not in a good way." Kate hugged him tight. "Don't you ever *ever* do that again. Do you hear me? You're too little to cook by yourself."

"But Miz Alice lets me…"

"And believe me, she's going to hear about it," Rick told him. "But at least she's there with you in case something happens. She would never let you cook on your own.

The stove is off-limits, both here and at my mother's. Do you understand?''

Joey turned wounded eyes to Kate, who'd been examining him for burns. ''Mommy, I was just—''

''It doesn't matter what your intentions were, Joey. Rick is right. The stove is off-limits.'' Her still-racing heart turned over at her son's misery, but she had to be strong. ''Now go upstairs and change your shirt.''

Kate watched Joey leave the kitchen like a defeated soldier, then she picked up her dropped crutch and straightened. Her panic for Joey receding, she now realized that her son had almost burned down Rick's house.

She turned to find him glaring at her.

Her heart plummeted. ''I'm sorry, Rick. You probably want us to leave now, so—''

''Just shut up.'' He turned to pick up the burned towel and wring it out.

''What?''

He slammed the towel into the garbage can and glowered at her. ''Do you have any concept of what just happened? And why?''

''Of course I do. My son almost burned down your house. If you hadn't come home when you did...'' She shivered. ''I can't tell you how sorry I am. I know it's my fault. I should've watched him more closely.''

''Oh, it's your fault, all right.'' He yanked the pan off the stove. ''But not because you left him alone. He's almost five. You should be able to trust him alone for fifteen minutes.''

She hobbled close to the sink. ''I'll clean everything up.''

''The hell you will.'' He poured the soup down the garbage disposal. ''This is your fault, Kate, but I doubt you realize how deep your guilt goes.''

''He's my son. That means I'm responsible for his actions.''

''He's your son, all right. Through and through. You've

taught him well. He's just as damned independent as you are. And it's probably going to kill him.''

She took a step back. ''What?''

''He tried to cook it himself. Now where the hell could he have got that notion into his head? Hmm? Could it possibly be from his 'just leave me the hell alone' mother?''

''I...'' Dear God. Were Rick's words true? Was the self-reliance she was teaching her son doing him more harm than good?

''Your attitude was hard enough to take when it was just endangering you. But now you've proved that it's endangering your son, as well. Is that what you want, Kate? Is that what you meant to do? Make your son so damned independent that he'll kill himself?''

Kate sat down hard on a breakfast nook chair. ''I had no idea...''

''Well, now you do.'' He opened the dishwasher and all but threw the pan on the bottom rack.

Kate felt as if he were throwing it at her. ''If you'll call a cab, we'll leave.''

''And just where the hell would you go?''

She swallowed hard and lifted a shoulder. ''It doesn't matter.''

He cursed vividly under his breath as he slammed the dishwasher closed. ''You're staying right here. God only knows what you'd do to the child if *you* didn't have some supervision.''

Knowing she deserved his words, she winced.

''Not only are you staying here, you're moving downstairs. I picked up another bed at Mother's.'' He started the dishwasher, then turned to face her. ''As for my working, I'm going to let you decide. Either I stay home until I feel reasonably sure you're able to take care of yourself or I hire a nurse.''

''A nurse? Do you know how much a nurse would cost?''

''No, but I'll be damned before I'll let a four-year-old

do a job meant for a nurse. Even though they released you from the hospital, you're still weak. You can't take care of yourself, and Joey can't, either. It's either a nurse or me. Your choice."

"But—"

"Your choice, Kate. Think about it while I go upstairs and check on Joey."

Kate stared after him. That was no choice. It would cost him money either way. She was so tired of thinking about how much she owed him, so tired of causing him trouble. Between her and Joey...

Was she really endangering her son by teaching him to be self-reliant? She'd always thought she was doing Joey a favor, teaching him young not to count on other people. Other people disappointed you just when you needed them most.

Except for Rick.

Kate was amazed that he hadn't kicked both of them out. Every time something happened that made her certain he'd bail on them, he surprised her.

She'd never met anyone like him. He seemed more determined to help her than she was not to be helped.

Rick walked in the door. "I'm sorry I overreacted. And I didn't mean to imply you're a bad mother. You're not. But he scared me half out of my mind."

Again Kate was humbled by his reasonableness. "You didn't overreact. He scared me, too."

Rick nodded. "I know."

Their eyes met and a look sizzled between them. A moment of understanding, a connection regarding the hazards of parenthood.

Kate dragged her gaze away. She was imagining things again. Joey was *her* son, not Rick's. "Where is he?"

"He's fine. He'll be down in a minute." He crossed his arms over his chest and leaned against the counter. "I'm sorry, but the choice still stands. Me or a nurse. Which is it?"

Kate didn't know how much he would lose if he didn't go to work, but she had an idea how much a live-in nurse would cost. She couldn't cost Rick any more real money, money she'd only have to repay.

She took a deep breath, but her voice was small as she said, "You."

He blinked. "What was that? I didn't hear you."

"You," she said louder.

He started to smile, but caught himself. He gave her a curt nod instead. "Good choice. Now, what would like for lunch? More soup or Alice's chicken salad sandwiches?"

"I can—"

"Pardon me?"

She dropped her gaze. "The chicken salad would be nice."

"Another good choice." With a smile he turned and opened the bread box.

Chapter Seven

The next morning Kate woke to the sound of the refrigerator door closing in the kitchen next to her makeshift bedroom. The tapping of little feet after that told her it was Joey, no doubt getting the milk for his cereal.

Frowning, she thought about what had happened the day before. Maybe Rick was right. Maybe she expected too much of her son.

She swung her heavy leg cast off the bed and sat up. "Joey?"

"Yeah, Mommy?" he called.

"You haven't poured the cereal yet, have you?"

"No, ma'am."

"Put it away, then. I'll scramble you an egg for breakfast."

"Yes, ma'am!"

She smiled at the smile in his voice, then rose awkwardly. After indulging in as much of a stretch as she could manage with a cast on her leg and arm, she pulled the nightgown off and reached for clean underwear.

She only had three sets, which made for frequent washing, but that was better than having Alice spend more money.

Shaking her head, Kate held up the lacy red push-up bra and see-through string bikini panties that matched. She could only imagine what Alice's relationship with her husband had been like for her to buy such impractical, sexy lingerie. It was certainly a far cry from the six-pack cotton panties that Kate bought at Wal-Mart.

Oh, well. She had to make do with what she had.

Stifling a yawn, she donned the underwear, blessing Alice for at least buying a front-closure bra. Getting the panties over the cast always took a little time, but Kate soon had them in place.

As she was reaching for her sweater, she heard a creak in the hall.

She glanced up just as Rick hit the bottom of the stairs...right outside the dining room.

"Good morn—" He stopped dead when he saw her.

Kate froze, both with shock—he was never downstairs this early—and at the look on his face.

He stared at her body, clad only in the sexy, revealing, red lingerie. His gaze ate her up, as if she was a stick of cotton candy.

She should be horrified, to be so exposed. But she wasn't. The warm surprise and obvious pleasure in his face made her feel like the most beautiful creature on earth.

"Kate..." Her name floated on a reverent breath as he took a step toward her.

"Mommy, can I make the toast?"

Joey's call broke the spell.

Rick gasped and drew back his hands, which had automatically reached for her. "I'm sorry. I didn't know you were..." He spun about. "Damn. I'm sorry."

Kate watched him bolt from the room. Galvanized from her shock, she snatched up the blue cotton sweater and dragged it over her head.

What was wrong with her, just standing there letting him

look his fill? When had she become so shameless? And what did he think of her, that she wore such seductive underwear?

Then an even worse possibility occurred to her. Did this mean she and Joey now had to leave? Dear God, where would they go?

Dressed, she made her way slowly, reluctantly toward the kitchen.

When she walked in, Joey said, "Finally! You took so long, Rick's cooking the eggs."

As she slid her gaze toward the stove, Rick turned to her with a bland expression. "How do you like them? Scrambled or fried?"

"Umm. Scrambled is fine."

He nodded and turned back to the stove. "Joey, you finished with the toast yet?"

As Joey replied, Kate released the breath she'd been holding. Okay. So they were going to forget the awkward moment. Act as if it never happened.

Good. She could do that.

Relieved but at the same time vaguely dissatisfied, she hobbled toward the table.

"Mommy, give me all your nines."

"I hope you have some bait on your hook, little boy, because you have to *go fish*."

"Awww!" Joey picked up a card from the down-turned deck and added it to his hand.

Rick watched them with a smile. It was a hair past seven o'clock on a Friday night, and for the first time in years, he was having fun. In fact, he'd been having fun for the past two days, in spite of all the hard work.

The word *fun* made the sight yesterday of Kate clad only in the sexiest red underwear he'd ever seen flash across his mind, but he firmly shoved it back into the corner where he'd hidden it. He couldn't think of her that way. It didn't matter that she was built like a goddess, with a waist that curved in from round hips he wanted to pull against his—

Yanking his mind back to the moment, Rick concentrated on the cards in his hand and on the reason he'd been enjoying *wholesome* fun.

After his and Kate's understanding the day after he'd brought her home, there hadn't been any more disagreements. Oh, there'd been moments when a bulldog expression had come over her face, but she'd swallowed her obstinacy and let him do what he needed to do. Which wasn't any more than he had to, and certainly nothing intimate.

Damn it.

"Earth to Rick."

Shaking off his thoughts, Rick became aware of four eyes watching him expectantly.

"My turn again?" He glanced at his cards. "Kate, give me all your queens."

Rolling her eyes, she handed over two cards, then peered over her shoulder at the kitchen behind her.

"What do you need?" he asked.

"I was just seeing if you had mirrors installed on the cabinets." She smiled wryly. "That's the third time you got me."

He grinned as he pulled out the two queens he already had and made a small pile on the table in front of him. "Maybe I'm psychedelic."

"Psy-ca-what?" Joey asked.

"Psychedelic," Rick answered with a straight face. "It means I'm covered with graffiti and all kinds of weird art inspired mostly by—"

"Rick means psychic, baby," Kate explained to her son. "He's saying he can read people's minds."

"He can?" The boy turned to Rick. "You can? Read mine!"

Rick placed his fingertips on his forehead and closed his eyes. "You're thinking... Let me see... I've got it. You're thinking you'd like another bowl of chocolate chocolate chip ice cream.''

"Oh, yeah!''

"Wait a minute.'' Kate held up her good hand. "Were you really thinking that, Joey?''

Joey thought about the question a second, then asked carefully, "If I say yes, can I have some?''

Rick laughed. "Good answer, little guy.''

Kate sent him a withering look, then glanced at the clock on the oven. "I don't know. Another hour and it's your bedtime.''

Rick slid from the window seat he shared with Joey. "Then we'd better eat it now, hadn't we?''

"I'll help.'' Joey jumped down and followed Rick across the room.

"I'll get the ice cream and bowls. You get three spoons.''

"Okay.'' Joey raced for the cabinet beside the stove.

"If I didn't know better, I'd say you were trying to fatten me up,'' Kate said.

As he opened the freezer door and pulled out the ice cream, Rick glanced over to see that she'd turned sideways in the chair so she could watch them.

She wore a blue jean skirt and a white cotton sweater that fitted her upper body as if it had been knit around her. He hadn't been able to think about much else all day. It was another of the outfits Alice had purchased for Kate in her never-ending shopping spree. Another of Alice's guerrilla matchmaking tactics.

Like that damn red bra and panties. Hell. It didn't help his peace of mind to know exactly what Kate looked like underneath her clothes.

With difficulty he forced his gaze away from the cleavage Kate probably didn't know she was showing. "It's not as though you couldn't stand to gain a few pounds.''

"Like your women fat, do y—''

Because she'd cut herself off, he glanced back over to

see her staring at the floor, a bright red flush splashed across her cheeks.

Then he caught the suggestion in her words. His women. Her choice of words implied she was one of them.

Heat surged upward. If she were, nights such as this could go on forever. He'd never have to face an empty house again. He'd never again be lonely.

Plus—and this was a *big* plus—he'd have Kate in his bed. Red underwear and all.

The heat crested in his brain, ripping through the deadwood of his thoughts, leaving just one—he wanted her.

"You want me to find the scoop, Rick?"

"What?" Joey's mundane question brought Rick's mind leaping from the flames. "Oh. That's okay. It's right here in the drawer."

"You sure are a space cadet tonight," Kate commented.

"Sorry." He pulled open the drawer and pulled out the scoop.

Joey grinned up at him. "You gonna join Star Fleet, Rick?"

"Ha-ha. Very funny." He smeared chocolate ice cream across Joey's nose. "There. Now you look like a Klingon."

The boy giggled, then puffed himself up and stuck his elbows in the air. He stalked to the table and growled at his mother. "It's a good day to die."

With a tiny gasp at Joey's words, Kate reached out and gathered him in her arms for a hug. "Don't say that, baby. Please."

"Aww, Mommy, it's what Klingons say 'fore they fight. You're s'posed to be afraid."

As he dipped into the ice cream, powerful emotions swept through Rick.

He knew exactly what Kate was thinking—that she'd come too close to dying for the Klingon phrase to be amusing. On the other hand, he was bust-his-buttons proud of Joey because using it demonstrated his keen intelligence. He'd introduced Joey to *Star Trek* reruns, and the youngster insisted on watching the show every day they could. The boy had picked up on nuances of plot and interspecies relationships quicker than many adults.

At that moment Rick felt closer to these two people than he'd ever felt to anyone. The three of them felt like a family, felt like what he'd been craving all his life. They needed him—for the moment, at least—and being needed was the most satisfying feeling he'd ever experienced.

But how long would his fantasy-come-true last? Until Kate's casts came off? Would she pack up their things then, and leave him?

Rick felt the intoxicating feelings pop around him like soap bubbles. He was becoming too accustomed to having Kate and Joey here, filling his house with arguments and laughter. He couldn't do that. If he did, the house would be unbearably lonely when they left. And they *would* leave, because Kate had made it clear that she was determined never to need anyone.

Even him.

"Your hair is so cute!" Alice tossed smiles at Kate as she drove.

Kate patted her curls. At least, what there was left of them. She'd complained about her shaggy tresses yesterday when Alice came to take Joey to a movie, so Alice had insisted on taking Kate to her hairdresser today.

"There's nothing there. I feel like one of those basketball players who shaves his head."

Alice chuckled. "Well, there isn't much, but short looks wonderful on you. So few women have the face for such a short cut."

"Thank you. I guess Emmy didn't have much to work with, did she? And it will grow."

"Yes, hair tends to do that." Alice beamed at her across the car. "Rick and Joey are going to be so surprised."

"Shocked is more like it." Kate couldn't stop touching

the extremely short curls. "Joey's never seen me with anything but long hair."

"And Rick's never seen you with anything but half-and-half."

"Yes, well, what Rick thinks doesn't matter. All that matters is that it looks presentable enough to get me a job."

Alice threw a troubled glance at her. "You don't like Rick?"

"Well…sure I do. I mean, what's not to like? He's helped me so much. And so have you. I want you to know that Joey and I appreciate all you've done, and I'm going to repay you every penny you've—"

"No, no, no. I wish you'd stop talking like that. I feel as if I'm the one who should be repaying you."

"Repaying me? What for? I haven't done anything but cost you and your son a lot of time and money."

Alice sighed. "Oh, my dear. You've done far more than you know. You've saved Rick's life."

Kate blinked. "Saved his life? How? I didn't even know he was sick."

"He's not sick. It's just… Well… This is going to take a bit of explanation. There's a Starbucks just ahead. Let's stop in for some coffee, all right? Can you manage getting in and out of the car one more time?"

"I've become quite adept with the crutches the past week." Kate hesitated. She knew she shouldn't ask, shouldn't even care, but she'd been dying to know. "Is this…is it about his wife?"

Alice nodded. "Her name was Stacy. But let's wait until we get settled, dear. All right?"

"Sure."

Kate didn't even fuss when Alice bought her a mocha latte and pastry. Rick had made cryptic statements, and Kate had been too polite to pry. But if Alice was offering the information…

"They met their first year in high school," Alice began when they were settled in a comfortable booth. "Rick always said that he fell in love with Stacy the minute he laid eyes on her. And he must've, because he never dated anyone else. They never broke up, even for a few days. Never even had a good, old-fashioned, knock-down, drag-out argument, for all I know.''

''What did she look like?'' Kate asked. ''Rick doesn't have any pictures around.''

''No. He had enough reminders as it was.'' Alice sipped her coffee thoughtfully. ''Stacy was very pretty, but in a different way from you. She had dark hair and dark brown eyes. She was a few inches shorter than you, and a little bustier. She'd gained a lot of weight with the pregnancy, though, so I think it would have been difficult for her to get her figure back. Though Rick wouldn't have cared. He was in his element. My Rick was born to be a family man. He loved taking care of Stacy, and she loved having him take care of her. She took good care of him, too. Stacy was an excellent cook. Better than I am, and I'm good.''

Kate smiled at Alice's good-natured bragging even as she felt pangs of jealousy. But that was ridiculous: not only did Kate have no desire to replace Stacy, but the woman had been dead for three years. Which brought up the most important subject. ''She died in an auto accident, right?''

Alice nodded sadly.

''What happened?''

The older woman sighed. ''Rick and Stacy were coming home from the home of some friends of theirs from church. Rick was driving. He'd stopped at a red light, then started forward when the light turned green. A car ran the red light. Ran it going about twenty miles over the speed limit. Alcohol involved. You know how it is. Anyway, it slammed into Stacy's side.''

Knowing Rick the way she did, Kate felt like crying—for him, and for the love he'd lost. ''Did she die instantly?''

Alice shook her head. ''That would've been a blessing. No, her brain was dead but her body lived on, at least it did on all the machines they had her hooked up to. She was five months pregnant and lost the baby right off, of course. It was a boy. It took two more days of hoping, but Rick finally gave permission for the doctors to turn the machines off.''

Chills raced across Kate's skin. ''From what I've gathered, Rick blames himself for Stacy's death, just like he blames himself for what happened to me. But neither one of them was his fault.''

''You're right. With Stacy, he blames himself for not looking both ways before entering the intersection.''

''And with me he thinks he wouldn't still have been in the middle of the road if he hadn't been so tired.''

Alice nodded. ''After Stacy died, he threw himself into Data Enterprises. Worked twelve, sixteen hours a day. Not because he needed the money. He worked himself to exhaustion so he could forget, so he'd be tired enough to sleep at night without seeing his wife's pale, dying face in his dreams.''

''Oh, Alice.''

''When you ran into him, he'd put in a seventy-hour week, and it was only Thursday.'' Alice watched her intently. ''Can you see why I said you've saved Rick's life?''

Kate frowned down at her cup as she ran a finger around the rim. ''All I've done is keep him from going to work.''

''Exactly.''

''I don't understand.''

The older woman leaned forward. ''I haven't seen Rick this animated in over three years. You and Joey are showing him that there's life out there. He still wants a family, and he's certainly young enough to have one. He's just afraid, I think. Afraid to start over, when Stacy was all he knew. Afraid of losing another family, too, probably.''

''Alice, Joey and I are not Rick's family.''

Even as she said them, the words felt like a lie. For the past week the three of them had seemed like a family…or at least, what she'd always thought a close family would be like. And Rick was a big part of it. He helped Joey sound out words when he was reading. With her he discussed events they'd seen on the news. He cooked dinner and took out the garbage and...and sent long heated looks her way.

But he never acted on them. Never touched her intimately, never said a word out of line.

Kate pushed away her sudden disappointment.

Alice took a long sip of her coffee.

"We're not." Which one of them was Kate trying to convince? And why did she suddenly feel so depressed?

Her hair. She could blame it on her hair.

"If you're not, it doesn't matter. You've brought him back to life and, hopefully, he'll never want to hide in his work again. So don't you dare talk to me about paying anything back. I won't take it. You're worth every cent I've spent on you...and more." Alice reached across and grasped Kate's hand. "You've given me back my son, Kate. Something no one else has been able to do. For that, you're worth your weight in gold."

Kate didn't like this kind of talk. She pulled her hand away. "You're making me sound like some kind of saint, and I'm not. I haven't done anything, except lie in a coma for two weeks. And now I sit around the house while he does everything."

Alice shrugged. "I don't know what it is you've done, dear. But whatever it is, please, please, please keep it up."

All afternoon Kate thought about Alice's comments, and that evening as she watched Rick and Joey play Chinese checkers on the coffee table in the living room, she reached a conclusion.

She'd been wondering all along what Rick expected in payment for everything he'd done. He'd almost convinced her that there were no strings attached.

But now Kate realized that Rick was using her to atone for what he thought he did to his wife.

Their situations weren't dissimilar. Stacy went to the

hospital for injuries sustained in a traffic accident in which he was driving—just like Kate. Stacy lay unmoving, hooked up to machines—just like Kate. Stacy had been pregnant with a son—Kate had a son.

The first one—the one he loved—died. But Kate didn't.

That's where the similarities ended…but that's where the reward lay for Rick. He'd expiated his guilt by taking care of Joey and Kate.

That's why he'd been so insistent on paying the hospital bill until the insurance could be straightened out. That's why he'd been so conscientious about taking care of Joey. That's why he let his mother buy clothes for them both, and that's why he'd been adamant about bringing her to his house until she recovered—and what she wanted be damned.

He wasn't doing these things for Kate. He was doing them for Stacy.

Kate's brows lowered. But her logic was sound, wasn't it?

"Does having no hair give you a headache?"

Kate blinked at Rick, who grinned at her from the other side of the coffee table. "Pardon me?"

"You're frowning so hard I thought you might be missing your hair."

"Very funny. I'm fine."

His smile faded. "Seriously. Do you need a pain reliever?"

"I'm fine. Really. Go on with your game."

He nodded, glanced down at the board then back up again. "I'm just kidding about your hair, by the way. I like it."

"Yeah, Mommy. I like it, too."

"Thank you." She reached for her crutches. "I'm going to get a glass of water. Anyone want anyth—"

Rick bounced to his feet. "I'll get it for you."

"No, you won't." She hauled herself upright. "I need to visit the powder room, too. Go on and play."

She could feel his warm brown eyes on her as she left the room, but she knew he wasn't watching her. He was watching a ghost.

Chapter Eight

Pausing at the door to the living room, Rick watched Kate, unnoticed.

She was ignoring the news on the television as she thumbed through a magazine. Her left arm—freed from the cast that day—moved deliberately but without any apparent pain as she turned the pages.

It seemed natural to see her sitting on his deep-green leather couch. She looked as if she belonged. He could picture himself walking behind the couch and leaning over as she lifted her face for his kiss.

When he actually started forward to oblige, Rick shook away the image and gave purpose to his movement by announcing, "Dinner is served."

Kate's face lit for the briefest instant, the way it always did when he joined her. There were times when he made an excuse to leave the room, just so he could come back and see her expression. It made him feel wanted.

Just before she dropped her gaze to reach for her crutches, however, her expression changed from pleasure to concern. "I wish you would've let me help you. Now that my cast is off, both hands are free."

Her words made him resist the temptation to help her to her feet. The damned old I-can-do-it-myself syndrome again. "Let your arm rest for a day. Get it used to being out of the cast."

She lifted herself from the couch easily, proving that she was gaining strength every day. "Whatever you cooked smells wonderful. I've heard men like you exist, but I've never met one who can cook not just edible but delicious food."

He felt like a dog having its fur stroked as he walked beside her toward the kitchen. He would've set dinner in the dining room tonight, but couldn't since it still served as her bedroom. "If bachelors don't learn to cook, they either starve or live on hamburgers."

"There are real restaurants, you know."

"But you have to sit there...alone...while nearly everyone around you is paired off. If you eat at home, you can watch TV. At least there's another voice in the room."

She paused in the hall and studied him with an odd expression.

He met her gaze steadily. Her ice-blue eyes were clear crystals. She seemed puzzled, and worried somehow.

"What's the matter?" he asked.

As if just realizing she was staring, Kate glanced away. "Nothing."

A possibility landed on Rick as softly as a butterfly. He stood perfectly still, not wanting to scare it away, as she moved down the hall.

Kate had been lost in thought about him...just as he'd been lost in thought about her just moments ago. Were they the same kind of thoughts?

He glanced up the stairs, his mind filling with ways they could be filling the hours until Joey came home from the birthday party Alice had taken him to...satisfying hunger of an entirely different nature.

Noticing she'd reached the kitchen, he hurried to join her.

She entered only to stop in midstride as she rounded the kitchen island. She leaned against crutches set forward and gaped at the elaborate table he'd set—complete with Stacy's wedding china and silverware. Even candles.

"What…" She stopped to clear her raspy voice. "What's the occasion?"

Gratified that she'd noticed, Rick walked over and pulled out her chair. "Celebrating you getting your cast off, of course. And I thought for once we could eat like real grown-ups since Joey is out with Mom."

"Oh." Kate swung forward. "You didn't have to go to all this trouble."

"I know. I thought it would be fun." He took her crutches and leaned them against the wall close by, then carried the hot dishes over while she watched. "It's nothing fancy. Beef tips with noodles, asparagus spears and a frozen cherry cobbler for dessert."

"Still frozen?"

"Very funny." He took his place on the window seat. "Dig in."

Since nothing was said as they filled their plates, Rick's mind was free to wander. It quickly found the path he'd already started down—wondering if Kate was attracted to him.

If he were honest with himself, he'd have to finally admit that he'd been attracted to her even when she lay in a coma. There was just something about her, some connection he'd felt from the moment he'd lifted her from her demolished car. As she grew stronger day by day, so did his attraction.

What if he said something? How would she react? Would she remind him that when he'd brought her to his home, he'd sworn it was just to give her time to heal? Or would she—

His thoughts scattered like butterflies when she reached for her crutches. "Where are you going?"

"To get the salt and pepper."

The butterflies vanished with a poof. Disgusted both at having his fantasies interrupted and by her refusal to ask for help, he slid to his feet, separating her from her crutches.

Grabbing the salt and pepper, he set them on the table, hard. "Why can't you—just once—ask for something? That's what I'm here for. That's why I've stayed home from work. I've had to anticipate your every need because if I don't, you'll be killing yourself trying to get or do it yourself."

Her chin lifted. "And that would put you back at square one, wouldn't it?"

He blinked. "What does that mean?"

She stared at him, looking as if she wanted to tell him exactly what was on her mind. Instead, she frowned fiercely and glanced away. "Nothing."

He grabbed her chin and forced her to look at him. "You're not going to get away with a cryptic statement like that. What the hell do you mean?"

Her blue eyes blazed. "I mean that it doesn't matter whether or not I ask for help because you're not helping me."

"Not helping… Then what the hell am I doing?"

"Oh, you're helping, all right. But not me."

"Who am I helping, if not you? I don't see anyone else in the room."

"Stacy."

"Stacy?" For an instant the name meant nothing to him. When it registered, he demanded, "What does she have to do with anything?"

"She has everything to do with it. At least to you." He felt her chin tighten under his fingers. "When you look at me, you don't see *me*. You see Stacy. When you do something for me, you're not helping *me*. You're helping her. Or rather, you're helping yourself get over her."

Shocked by her words, Rick didn't resist when she jerked her chin away.

How could she read him so well? Was the connection he'd felt from the beginning so strong that she could sense his thoughts? Know his motivations?

The possibility scared him...yet thrilled him at the same time. He'd never felt this close to anyone.

He focused on her lovely face. She stared down at the table, the scar on her temple vivid against her pale skin.

If she could read his mind, what she'd read was on time delay because the motivation he'd started out with had changed. Somewhere along the way Stacy had faded into a memory. Not forgotten, but no longer a source of daily pain.

"Not see you?" he asked. "A man would have to be blind."

She turned to him with wide eyes. Flinching for a brief second as he lifted his arms, she then sat perfectly still as he gently laid a hand on either side of her face. "You're wrong, angel Kate. So very wrong. Stacy has barely crossed my mind for the past week, which is just one of the miracles you've performed."

She swallowed hard, but didn't look away. "I'm not an angel."

He smiled. "Looks like an angel...talks like an angel..." Lowering his head, he softly touched his lips to hers. The contact, meant as a casual caress, astounded him. The sudden roaring in his ears and breathlessness in his chest made him feel as if he were being flown straight to heaven. He didn't want the feeling to end, but somehow he found the strength to pull away.

As he drew back, her breath caught.

Blood raced through his veins like a video of race cars on fast forward. His voice was heavy, thick and deep. "Tastes like an angel."

Her eyes turned an incredible shade of blue.

Mesmerized by the color, he stared down into them.

"Are you surprised, angel Kate? Are you shocked by my desire? I want you, you know. More than any woman I've ever known. Even Stacy."

"Rick..." Her voice was raspy and sexy and sweet.

The evidence of her own desire drew him close again—like a butterfly to the nectar of a beautiful flower. "Once more, angel. Just one more kiss..."

Her gaze dropped to his lips. "Yes."

One hand slid into her short curls to support her head as he pulled her chin up. *Gentle* never entered his mind this time. His mouth took hers hungrily, deeply, with a savage need that had built insidiously inside him as he'd tried to deny what he felt.

She whimpered and opened her mouth as his tongue demanded full access. Her arms slipped around his back, her hands rubbing the taut muscles as her tongue joined his in a dance so searingly seductive, he dropped his arms to her waist to lift her to her feet, fully intending to carry her to the nearest bed.

The phone blared from the wall across the kitchen.

They broke apart and stared at each other in incomprehensible surprise, breathing deeply to cool the fire drumming through their veins.

"It's probably Joey," Kate said on the third ring.

"Yes." Rick smoothed a curl back from the scar on her temple. "Joey. Right." He straightened. "I'll get it."

Rick caught the portable phone on the fifth ring, just before the answering machine would've picked up. "Hello?"

"Hey, Rick! It's me," Joey said brightly.

Rick's tense muscles relaxed. "Hey, little guy. Have fun at the party?"

"I won a prize! A baseball. Will you teach me how to pitch?"

"Well, I was always better at catching, but we can work on it. You ready to come home?"

"Uh-huh. Miz Alice says she'll bring me. Is Mommy there?"

"Sitting right here. Hang on."

Rick handed Kate the phone, then slipped onto the window seat. He barely listened to her conversation as his mind raced with the implications of what he'd done. He'd tried to seduce a woman who was not only under his care, but who hadn't recovered from her injuries. She still wore a cast on her leg, for God's sake.

How low could one man stoop?

Kate said goodbye, punched the off button on the phone, then placed it on the table beside her untouched plate. She sat for a moment staring down at it.

He'd scared her to death. Damn. What was he thinking?

The better question was—what was he thinking *with?* The answer to that was still throbbing painfully.

He shifted on the window seat. "Kate, I'm—"

"I don't—"

They cut themselves off, and their eyes met in surprise. Rick seized the initiative. "I'm sorry. What I did was unforgivable."

Her gaze dropped. "Not unforgivable."

His breath caught, but he forced it out of his lungs. "Incredibly stupid, then. I swore I never had any intention of you repaying me for anything I've done, especially sexually. And that's true. The kiss wasn't about that. All right?"

"All right." Her voice was soft but intense.

"Payment of any kind never even entered my mind, believe me. All I wanted—" He drove a hand through his hair. "Well, to be perfectly frank, all I wanted...want is you."

Her gaze lifted, then dropped. "I kissed you, too, you know."

His eyes squeezed tightly, as if he could shut out the image. As if. "Yes, unfortunately for my good intentions, I do know that."

"Rick—"

"But I promise I will not act on it." He leaned back on the cushions of the window seat. "Not only are you under my care, you haven't fully recovered from your injuries. I'd be the worst kind of man if I started anything. Besides..."

"Yes?"

He hesitated. He'd already admitted his desire, might as well lay out his apprehensions, too. This wasn't easy, though. He hadn't discussed his feelings with anyone in a long time. "From what I think I know about you, and what I do know about me, we're not very compatible. You insist on having a career. I want a wife who will stay home and take care of the family."

She frowned. "That's Neanderthal thinking. Do you know how many women work outside the homes these days?"

"I know, and I think the children suffer for it. I think families suffer."

"Typical male logic. Keep the woman ignorant, barefoot and pregnant. Reverse the roles. How would you like to wake up every morning, knowing the most important thing you have to do that day is clean the toilet? Plus, when a woman has a career, she's never stuck in an intolerable situation. She can support herself and her kids if she has to. And with the divorce rate these days, a lot of them have to."

"You're only proving my point. We're not compatible." He shrugged. "I'm not going to apologize for how I am. I need a woman who likes being taken care of, because it's what I love to do. I'm sure you've figured that out by now. But you resent it when I so much as get you a glass of water."

"I never asked you to help me, did I? And I certainly didn't ask for...compatibility."

"No, you haven't asked for anything. And won't if you can possibly avoid it." His eyes narrowed. "But you can't deny we're compatible sexually. I know I started it, but you were doing as much kissing as I was."

Her frown deepened. "I know."

To keep his hands to himself after *that* admission, Rick pondered her aversion to charity. His Southern upbringing forbade prying, but his curiosity ate through it. "Something had to have happened to you at some point in your life for you to be this…pathological about people helping you."

She shrugged jerkily. "It wasn't any one thing. Just…the way I grew up."

"Can you—" He stopped himself. But since his hint didn't get him the information he sought, he had to ask her outright. As a Southern gentleman, he was already damned for the hint. Might as well be damned for the question. "Will you tell me about your childhood?"

She searched his face, as if gauging the depth of his interest.

"Please," he said. "I'd really like to know."

She dropped her gaze to her untouched plate. "I wouldn't know where to begin."

"Why not like David Copperfield? I was born…"

She fingered the tines of her fork nervously. Just when he thought she wouldn't, she started talking. Her words came hesitantly at first, reluctantly. "I was born in Nashville. My father played in a country band. My mother was a waitress at one of the nightclubs where he played. That's how they met."

"Were you their oldest child?"

"I was their only child. My father left before I was two."

"Just left?" Rick knew there were men who did this, but he couldn't understand abandoning a wife and a beautiful daughter.

Kate nodded. "Apparently. I don't remember him at all." She drew a deep, shaky breath. "Anyway, my mother wasn't too good in the job department. We lived from hand to mouth, when we lived together at all."

"She abandoned you, too?" This was totally beyond his comprehension.

"No. Not really. But we ended up living on the street several times, and after a few months the child welfare people would find us and take me to live in a foster home. I've heard there are good, caring, kind people who become foster parents, but that wasn't my experience. I lived in five homes, in all. In three of them I worked like a slave for the little I got. In one, the man sold drugs on the side. The other couple was too busy to care."

"Damn." Rick leaned back. "No wonder you didn't want the state to get hold of Joey."

"Exactly. I promised myself I would never put him in that kind of situation. I promised him I would always take care of him. Now here I am…" Her voice choked and she looked away.

Rick reached across the table and placed his hand over Kate's. Hers was ice-cold. "Joey is in no danger of going to a foster home. You took care of him by asking me to take care of him. See? Good things *can* happen when you ask people for help."

"Yes, but you were a perfect stranger. I didn't know if you'd be any different from the foster homes I stayed in."

He squeezed her hand. "Yes, you did. You knew. Didn't you?"

Her eyes widened and delved into his.

The connection he'd felt all along sparkled between them. "You feel it, too, don't you?"

"Feel…what?"

"There's something between us, Kate. And it's more than sexual. It was there from the night we ran into each other. You knew instinctively that I'd take good care of Joey. And I felt…I don't know. It's like you were speaking to me—in my head—while you were in the coma."

She dropped her gaze and pulled her hand from his. "I don't know what you mean."

"Kate—"

"You said we aren't compatible."

Rick leaned back in frustration and couldn't help asking, "What about Joey's father? Were you compatible with him?"

She turned her face farther away. "Obviously not."

"Why 'obviously'? Where is he? Why isn't he helping you?"

She laughed derisively. "Mitch help anyone? He was selfish to the core."

"Where is he?"

She shrugged and finally looked at him. "I don't know and I don't care. I haven't seen him since I told him I was pregnant."

"He abandoned you?"

She nodded. "When I told him I was pregnant, he told me to have an abortion. Then he left and never came back."

Rick tamped down the anger welling up inside. "Were you married?"

"No. We were both in school. I was a year away from a degree in accounting when I had to quit and get a job so I could support myself and Joey."

"What's his last name, Kate? We'll find him and make him help you."

"No." Her eyes narrowed. "I don't want his help."

"There are laws concerning deadbeat fathers."

"I don't care." She shivered. "I don't want to ever see him again."

"Kate…"

"Joey will be home soon." She picked up her fork.

"Why can't you—"

"No, Rick."

Frustrated even more, he watched Kate poke at the food on her plate.

The good news was that he understood her better now, understood why she was so determined to do things for herself. He'd probably be the same way if he'd had the childhood she had, shoved into foster care and treated like an indentured servant…forced to repay the people who'd taken her in with hard labor. Then she was abandoned by the father of her child the way her own father had abandoned her.

Damn.

What made men do that? He couldn't understand anyone who didn't want to support their own children, who didn't want to live with them day by day, watching them grow, hearing their baby laughs, drying their tears, feeling their hugs. And Joey was such an exceptional boy, bright, happy, inquisitive.

Rick ran a hand back through his hair.

Kate had no family, no support, nothing to fall back on. He was amazed she'd gotten this far. Amazed that she'd raised such a wonderful child. Amazed by her resourcefulness, her determination, her strength.

What he now knew about Kate made him want to take care of her and Joey more than ever. That was the bad news. The need to keep her in his life—safe and warm and worry free—was so strong it frightened him.

He was afraid he was falling in love with her.

The signs were there. He wanted her, and he wanted to take care of her. Having Kate and Joey around made his house ring with life, made him feel needed, gave purpose to his days—everything he'd craved for the past three years.

The only problem was, Kate made him feel like a monster every time he tried to help her. There were moments when he actually felt guilty for enjoying having them there.

"I just want to make one thing perfectly clear," he said.

She glanced at him guardedly. "Yes?"

He picked up his fork. "You do not have to do anything in this house for me or for Joey or for anyone that you don't want to do. I do not expect you to repay me in any way. Any way at all. You don't have to clean. You don't have to cook. And above all, you don't have to…to… Oh, hell. You don't have to sleep with me. Is that clear?"

Kate nodded briefly.

"I mean it, Kate."

"All right." She daintily cut a stalk of asparagus in three even pieces. Spearing the tip, she dipped it in the ranch dressing that was his shortcut to hollandaise and placed it in her mouth.

She was only eating, but to Rick her moves were sensual, enticing.

He tore his gaze away with a muttered curse and dug his fork into a beef tip. Lately everything she did was sensual and enticing. All she had to do was breathe, and he was panting after her.

He didn't know if he was in danger of falling in love or if he was already too far gone. But he knew one thing for sure—falling in love with Kate Burnett would be one of the stupidest things he'd ever done.

She didn't want what he had to offer, and he wouldn't settle for anything less. If he were smart, he'd stop the free-falling descent.

Right now.

Joey arrived home just as they finished dinner. Alice smiled when she saw the table laid out, then made an excuse to hurry home.

Kate knew what Alice was thinking, and the older woman was nearly right. If Joey hadn't called to tell them Alice was bringing him home, the two of them might have caught Rick and Kate in an extremely compromising situation. The dining room, which served as her bedroom and held the closest bed, was right inside the front door...to which Alice had a key.

Joey told them about his evening over cherry cobbler, but Kate's mind kept slipping back to what had nearly happened.

What was wrong with her? She'd been so seduced by Rick's kisses and straightforward declaration of desire, she would've followed him straight to her bed. Heck, she probably would've taken his hand and led him there.

One kiss and her resolve to never again become involved in a relationship that sapped her will had gone up in smoke. She knew exactly where heated, sexual relationships led. She'd traveled down that road with Mitch.

The only good thing that came out of her relationship with him was Joey. She'd worked hard for a college scholarship and had been a year away from an accounting degree, which would've assured her of a well-paying job almost anywhere. Instead, she'd had to quit school in order to support Joey, taking a job as an accounting clerk, which paid less than half what a CPA made. But at least it had provided them with food, shelter and insurance.

What would a relationship with Rick provide?

She watched him question Joey closely about winning the baseball. She had to admit he would be a wonderful father. *If* he stuck around.

Kate had learned the hard way that people in general— and men in particular—don't stick. Once you're the least bit of trouble, they get tired of helping you.

For some stupid, illogical reason, however, she believed Rick would stay.

Her gaze fell to her half-eaten cobbler.

There it was again, the connectedness. When he'd asked her if she felt it, too, she'd been so surprised that he felt it, she'd automatically denied it.

I do not expect you to repay me in any way. Any way at all.

She almost believed him. She wanted to believe him…but everything in her past had shown her that people didn't give for the sake of giving. They gave because they expected something in return.

What did Rick want? To have Joey as his son? Is that why he was seducing her?

She shivered. Could that have all been an act?

She didn't believe it. But then, she wasn't very good at

predicting the behavior of men when children were involved. She'd been blindsided when Mitch had turned his back on his own son.

"Are you cold?" Rick asked quickly.

He noticed everything.

"I'm fine." She picked up her spoon.

"You sure? I can turn up the heat."

Kate blinked, then decided his innuendo was unintentional. Definitely *not* disappointed, she lifted a spoonful of cherry cobbler. "You've done enough of that already, thankyouverymuch."

Catching *her* innuendo immediately, Rick stared at her—unblinking—until she felt that her cheeks must have turned as red as the cherries. Why had she gone and said something like that?

When Joey tugged on his shirtsleeve, Rick had to tear his gaze away.

Relieved she was no longer the focus of his attention, she watched him answer Joey's questions about baseball. Rick promised to take them to a Redbirds game this summer.

He was always doing something for them, and seemed happy to be doing it. But most important, he'd never—not once—mentioned payment of any kind. Was he sincere? Did he really mean it?

I mean what I say.

Maybe it was time to find out.

Chapter Nine

"I'm going into the kitchen," Rick announced an hour later. They sat in the living room watching television with Joey. Rick stood and looked more at Joey than her as he asked, "Can I get you anything?"

Now was the time.

Kate took a deep breath, then recognized it as a delaying tactic.

Rick had turned to leave the room when she forced herself to call, "Yes."

He pulled to a stop in the doorway and slowly turned. His deep-brown eyes shone with disbelief. "You're kidding."

Joey looked at her in shock. This would be a good lesson for him, too.

She ignored Rick's sarcasm. "Would you please bring me a glass of water?"

He lifted a wry brow. "Of course. Anything else?"

He was right. A glass of water wasn't a hard enough test of his willingness to do things for her without expecting payback. "Ice water, please."

"Is that it?"

"Yes. Thank you."

"Joey? Anything?"

Joey glanced at Kate.

She nodded. "It's okay, baby."

His face brightened, and he turned back around. "Can I have a glass of water, too, please?"

Rick's face softened. "Of course you can, little guy."

"Want me to help, Rick?" the boy asked.

"No. Stay and watch the program. I'll get it."

Several minutes later Rick returned with three glasses of ice water. He set two on coasters on the coffee table in front of himself and Kate, the other in front of Joey. "There you go."

They both chorused, "Thank you."

"No problem." Rick sat on the other end of the couch and stretched his arm along the back cushions.

Kate reached for the water and took a sip. She hadn't really wanted it. It had been a test.

She placed it back on the coaster.

Not much of a test, she had to admit. Water cost him nothing but a little time and effort. Okay, so the water was *her* test, not his. Just to see if she could get the words out.

And she did. Asking for water wasn't too hard. Now she needed to ask for something that would either cost money or effort, or both. That would be the real test for Rick.

After a trip to the bathroom a few minutes later, she had the perfect item. Something she was positive he would refuse to get.

Smiling, Kate returned to the couch and waited patiently for bedtime. After the show, she read Joey a bedtime story, then Rick took her son upstairs to tuck him in.

When he came back down, he said, "Is it all right if I go into work tomorrow? There's something I need to take care of."

"Of course." She couldn't believe he'd even asked.

"You don't need my permission. In fact, I'm glad you're finally going."

His smile was lopsided as he sat back down on the couch. This time he faced her instead of the television. "Glad to get rid of me for a few hours?"

"Not at all." She shrugged. "I've felt guilty for being so much trouble."

His brown eyes grew warm, like melted chocolate. "I like trouble."

Spoken in a low-pitched tone, his words made her heart beat faster, made her think about the kiss they'd shared.

He was doing this on purpose.

She concentrated on the test she'd planned. "I'm glad you said that, because I need something."

"You're asking me to do something for you?" He picked up the remote and changed the channel to CNN.

"What are you doing?"

"I want to see the flying pigs," he said without the barest hint of a smile.

"Ha-ha." She glanced away. She'd thought this particular test would be fun, but he was making it hard. "Flying pigs aside, I need something."

"What? Tell me." He seemed so darned eager.

"Well, I've just realized I…"

"Yes?"

"I need some…feminine products." There. She'd said it. She looked up to gauge his reaction.

"That time, huh? Do you need them tonight?"

It was Kate's turn to be surprised. Her request didn't seem to faze him. The only person she'd ever asked to purchase such personal items was Mitch, and he'd outright refused. "Umm, no. I'll be fine until tomorrow."

Yes, that would be better. There would be more people in the store during the daytime. More potentially embarrassing for him.

"All right. What kind do you prefer?"

Kate's eyes narrowed. "You're not actually going to buy

them for me, are you? You're going to ask Alice to get them.''

"I don't mind buying them. I used to get them for Stacy all the time. I just can't believe you're asking me to do it.''

Her chin lifted. "I can't exactly drive to the store myself…even if I had a car.''

"No, you can't. I'm happy to help. Really. I'll bring what you need at lunch. Just write down exactly what brand and style you want. There are so many different kinds these days.''

"You're not staying at work all day?''

He shook his head. "Just the morning, this first time. We'll see after that.''

"You want to see if I do anything stupid.''

He didn't deny it. "Joey will be here. If you do, he can call. I'm only ten minutes away.''

"I'll be fine,'' she insisted.

"Yes.'' His good mood vanished suddenly, and his face hardened. He looked away to pick up the book he'd been reading. "Aren't you always.''

Kate suddenly felt deflated. He made it obvious that she'd disappointed him, and she didn't have to wonder why.

She reached for her own book.

Well, that was just too bad. She'd asked for his help, hadn't she? What did he expect…that she'd say she couldn't live without him?

She *could* live without him. She'd been doing fine without his help for twenty-five years. She could do without it while he went to work for a few hours.

Geez.

Kate stared blindly at the unfocused words on the page.

She just wished that disappointing him didn't leave her feeling so…disappointed.

When Rick entered the condo a little after noon the next day, the first thing he noticed was the appetizing smell filling the hall. Following his nose to the kitchen, he found Kate leaning on a barstool at the island, stirring a pan of something chickeny and wonderful.

Joey sat at the table, practicing his writing. "Hey, Rick!"

"Hi, little guy." He set the brown bag of feminine supplies on the counter behind Kate. "What are you doing?"

She didn't turn. "Stirring soup."

"What soup? I didn't make any soup."

"I did."

"Why?"

"For lots of reasons. Because I'm bored. Because Joey's getting the sniffles and chicken soup is healing. But mostly because I wanted chicken soup."

"Kate, I told you last night you don't have to—"

"Just shut up, will you?" She replaced the lid on the pan and finally looked at him. "I'm going crazy sitting around the house with nothing to do."

"I told you that you don't have to cook or clean—"

"I know."

"You didn't believe me, did you?"

Her chin lifted, then checked as her gaze settled behind him. "Is that…?"

"Yes."

"Oh." Her slightly widened eyes met his. "Thank you."

"You're welcome."

Their gazes locked. Hers held questions he wanted to answer with his arms around her. But Joey was just a few feet away.

Thank God. Otherwise he might do something really stupid.

He *wanted* to do something really stupid.

Damn.

"I just wanted chicken soup," she said simply. "Really."

Though he wasn't convinced that she wasn't repaying him for purchasing her supplies, Rick let it go. "All right."

"It...um...needs a little salt, though. Could you hand it to me? Please?"

Rick picked up the salt shaker from the counter by the sink. When he turned to hand it to Kate, he caught her slight frown. Suddenly something dawned on him.

She was testing him.

The first emotion to hit him was annoyance. She didn't believe he—or anyone—would do something for her without expecting something in return.

Then Rick remembered how she came to have such a low opinion about people. Her distrust showed she had never experienced real love, where people did things for each other, gave to each other, for the pure joy of giving. Instead of feeling sorry for her, however, he was suddenly elated to realize he could be the one to...

No. He couldn't fall in love with her. Love had to be mutual, or a relationship wouldn't last. And love was based on trust.

Still...he could begin her education, couldn't he?

The best way would be to turn the tables on her. Since she was testing him to find out how much she could ask him to give without him demanding payment, then he would test her right back and see how much she would take without insisting on *re*payment.

If he were a betting man, he'd bet it wouldn't be much.

Over the next few days Rick wished he were a betting man and that he'd found someone foolish enough to cover the bet. Every time he did something for Kate, she paid him back immediately.

After he took Joey for a haircut, he found his sheets changed and the bathroom off the master bedroom sparkling. When he brought home a classy light-blue silk suit his mother had bought for Kate to wear on interviews, he found his laundry done, every missing button replaced, every split seam invisibly repaired.

Every night the delectable smells of supper wafted to his

nostrils as soon as he walked through the door. Kate's cooking was eye-rolling delicious, but he wondered where she found some of the ingredients. He'd never even thought about buying a Portabello mushroom, for God's sake.

It didn't take long for him to weasel out of Joey that Kate had a coconspirator and designated shopper—his mother. He wondered if Kate realized that Alice's motivations were just the opposite of her own. His mother wasn't helping Kate pay him back. He had no doubt Alice was working under the conviction that the way to a man's heart was through his stomach.

Probably the only reason his house hadn't been scrubbed from stem to stern was that Kate still had to deal with crutches.

On the other side of the situation were Kate's tests for him.

Would you please stop by the library and get some books for Joey? Could you call the people who've moved into my apartment and see if any mail has been delivered for me?

He wanted to chuckle every time she asked him to do something for her or Joey, but at the same time he wanted to set her down and give her lessons on determining a man's depth of caring. Her "tests" were not tests at all. They cost him nothing more than a little effort. The sad thing was, he knew Kate couldn't bring herself to cost him any more money.

Rick despaired of getting through to her. Then, on the day before he was taking her to get the cast off her leg, he came home early and handed her a stack of mail he'd retrieved from the people at the dingy apartment she'd lost. Thank God. He'd cringed to think of Kate and Joey living there.

Which made him realize the boy wasn't there. "Where's Joey?"

"Where else?" she murmured. "With Alice."

He wanted to ask how she planned to repay his mother for all she'd done, but he didn't. "That's right. He told me

Mom was taking him to a movie this afternoon. A new Disney film, isn't it?''

Her mind was clearly on sifting through her mail. "Hmm? Oh. No. It's been out several months, I think. It's at the second-run theater. They've been to all the first-run movies.''

Having picked up his own mail from the chest just inside the front door, he sat on the chair across from Kate and looked through it. It didn't take long to separate the bills from the junk. After he did, he glanced up to see Kate frowning at her mail.

"What's wrong?" he asked.

"There isn't anything from my insurance company. It's been over a month since the accident. Surely I should have something by now. I know I changed my address with them.''

"Something like what?" Rick carefully kept all expression off his face. She hadn't heard from her insurance company because he'd paid a lawyer to take care of the whole mess. Kate didn't need the hassle, and he didn't want to spare the time.

Kate lifted hands laden with envelopes in a confused shrug. "I don't know, some acknowledgment that they're working on getting things settled. They haven't even asked me to fork over my deductible.''

Rick sighed. He'd known he was going to have to tell her at some point.

It was another test for her. The biggest yet. But he wasn't optimistic about her passing it.

"Things are pretty much settled," he told her. "Just waiting on a check from the insurance of the driver who hit you.''

Her forehead wrinkled. "Settled how? I thought it was going to court.''

He sat forward. He refused to be defensive about this. "You don't have to worry about a thing. I hired a lawyer. He took care of everything.''

She let that sink in. "What about my deductible?"

"It was waived."

"Whose decision was that?"

"Mine. Your insurance company paid for the damage to my car. I told them to adjust the settlement check by the amount of your deductible."

"That was five hundred dollars."

"I know."

Instead of blowing up like he'd expected, Kate stared at him for long, silent moments. She didn't seem surprised, but she did seem incredulous. Then, to his surprise, her eyes began to fill with tears.

Distressed by her reaction, he got up and sat on the couch next to her. When he gathered her in his arms, she didn't resist. "I didn't do it to make you cry, beautiful Kate."

"I know." She sniffed. "You did it for her."

"Who?" Then he remembered. "Oh. Stacy."

"How much do you have to spend before you've paid her back, Rick? When are you going to stop feeling guilty?"

He rested his cheek against her silky hair, amazed to realize all the guilt was gone. As a matter of fact—as painful as it was to contemplate—he now knew Stacy died for a reason. If she was still alive, he'd never have come to know Kate and Joey. He would've missed having these two wonderful people in his life.

And that, he couldn't imagine.

It wasn't that he was glad that Stacy was no longer around. But he'd finally, after three long years, let her go. He'd finally—after three long, lonely years—let her go.

And he didn't feel guilty. He felt good...and he was certain Stacy did, too. Her ghost was finally free to return to Heaven.

The release he felt made powerful emotions sweep through him, and he hugged Kate tighter.

"I *have* stopped, Kate."

She lifted her head in surprise. "You have?"

He pushed back the curl over her scar. "You're right about my original motivations. When you lay there in the hospital, so pale and still, it was too much like what happened when Stacy died. All I could think about was doing everything I could to make you live, make you wake up and talk to me. When I arranged to pay for everything, guilt was what drove me."

She swiped the tears from her cheek. "What happened to change it?"

He smiled. "You woke up and fought me every step of the way. The more you resisted help, the more determined I became to help you."

"For Stacy, though."

"Maybe in the beginning. But for you, too. You fought so hard to get well. Stacy was a never a fighter. And I wanted to help for Joey's sake. I'd come to know him by then, and through him I came to know you. The closeness you have with your son is rare and precious. I wanted to preserve it at all cost."

She frowned. "Which is considerable."

"Not when you count the rewards. You and Joey have helped me, too, Kate. Don't you know that? I hope that we will always be friends."

Even as he said it, the word *friends* sounded out of place.

But friends is all they could ever be. They each wanted something different out of life, out of a relationship.

Kate's gaze fell to his chest. "I'm sure we will be. I can't see you letting Joey out of your life. And I can't see him letting go of you. You and Alice mean a lot to him."

"Joey's an extraordinary boy. So smart and inquisitive and capable."

"Well, I think so. But then, I'm prejudiced."

"You have reason to be." Rick pulled her back against him. "And your remarkable son means you're a remarkable mother."

She sighed and relaxed against his chest. "Thank you."

"It's true." He kissed the top of her hair, and for a long moment soaked in her warmth. "You surprised me."

"I did?"

"I thought you'd be yelling at me for hiring a lawyer, telling me in detail how you're going to pay me back."

"Would you let me pay you back?"

"No."

"Then what's the point? I've given up, Rick. You win the stubborn battle. There's no way I can possibly repay you and your mother for all you've done."

Rick's heart once again swelled with emotion. He was so proud of her. "Yes, there is."

She went still. "What?"

He smiled and cupped her chin. "Say 'Thank you.'"

Her wonderfully kissable lips curved in a rueful smile. "Thank you."

He felt as if he'd just been given the most priceless gift on Earth.

Chapter Ten

Rick entered the church social hall behind two boys excited just to be playing together. Joey and Mike had accompanied him out to Alice's car to retrieve a sweater for Kate.

The boys ran off toward the dessert table for another cookie.

Rick's eyes sought and immediately found Kate where he'd left her, sitting in a small circle of mostly older women, her crutches leaning against the wall behind her.

She talked quietly with Mike's mother, Andrea, who sat to Kate's left. She'd been two years behind Rick, growing up.

Alice sat on Kate's right, probably still telling the ladies on that side about her remodeling. When he'd left a few minutes ago to get the sweater, they'd been deep in a conversation about the pros and cons of light-colored carpet.

Other groups of men and women were scattered around the large concrete-walled room, eating the potluck feast spread across three folding tables and talking about politics, work, kids and life in general.

Rick hadn't attended the once-a-month Saturday night social since Stacy died. Too many memories, too many people reminding him of all he'd lost. Now he realized he'd missed it—the fellowship, the friends, the people who cared.

Kate glanced his way then and smiled.

Rick smiled back. She was the reason he was here. She and Joey had shattered the shell he'd crawled into after Stacy's death. They'd brought him back to life. His heart swelling with gratitude, he headed toward her.

"Thanks," she murmured as he wrapped the light silk sweater around her shoulders. "It was so warm today, I didn't realize it would be chilly tonight."

"Never know what the weather'll do this time of year," said Mrs. Pruitt, a feisty older woman on the other side of the circle.

"Plus these concrete floors stay cool," Andrea said. "Which is good in the summer, but can be miserable during the cold, cold days in winter."

"I guess I should've warned her, but I'd forgotten," Rick said as he returned Alice's keys to her.

"Men rarely feel cold the way women do," Andrea said.

"Paahh. If he'd come more often, he'd have known. There's enough ladies around here complaining about the cold in their bones," Mrs. Pruitt said.

"You're right, Mrs. Pruitt," Rick said with proper contrition. "I'll do better."

"And bring this lovely young lady and her adorable son with you." Mrs. Pruitt had never believed in subtlety. "It's time you rejoined life, as well as the church."

"Yes, ma'am." Rick leaned around Kate and took the empty plate from her lap. "Let me get you something else."

"No, thank you. I'm—"

"Get her some of Nina's homemade ice cream," Alice insisted. "She made peach this time."

"Sounds good. Would you like some, too?"

Alice straightened and ran a hand across her stomach. "No, dear. I need to watch my figure."

"And I don't?" Kate asked.

Alice waved a hand in Kate's direction. "You could use a little meat on your bones, dear. Right, Rick?"

"I think she's beautiful just the way she is," he answered. "But I'll get her some ice cream, anyway."

Frowning, Kate watched him walk across the room.

I think she's beautiful just the way she is.

What was that comment about? They were just friends, weren't they? Friends didn't make comments like that. Not any of the friends she'd had.

Rick was stopped several times by people he obviously knew and who knew him well. Alice had told her that Rick had grown up in this church. So had Stacy.

Kate wondered what such a life would be like, to have a group of people who knew everything about you—from the circumstances of your birth to how well you did in school to the state of your health. She and her mother had moved too often, always chasing better jobs which never seemed to be better...and never lasted very long.

Joey ran up to Rick then and tugged on his sleeve. When Rick looked down, Joey asked him something. Rick glanced across the room, then nodded. Joey sped off to join Mike on the other side of the room. Rick watched him, then turned back to the man he'd been speaking with.

The exchange was so much like a father would have with his son, Kate felt her heart contract. Joey needed this kind of relationship. He'd never known the caring strength of a father, something all boys needed and most took for granted.

All of this seemed so real, so normal. Rick seemed so real, so normal. At least, what she'd always considered normal.

Normal was something Kate and Joey had never had, no matter how hard she'd tried. Normal meant you had enough money to live on without scrimping to save for emergencies. Normal meant Joey needing new shoes did not qualify as an emergency. Normal meant you had a job and a place to live.

Normal was all she'd ever wanted.

Then she realized she and Joey lived in the nicest place they'd ever lived. They had more than enough to eat. More than enough shoes and clothes...really nice clothes.

Their lives were the most normal they'd ever been...all because of Rick.

Kate's eyes teared and her heart swelled with emotion. Gratitude. That's all it was, wasn't it?

Then she remembered the cast on her leg came off on Monday...hopefully. Would normal end for them then?

It was hard to believe she would leave Rick's house in a few days. It was hard to believe he'd let her.

Frowning at the strong connection she felt to this man, Kate dragged her eyes away and turned back around only to find every lady in the little circle watching her with knowing smiles.

"Can we say 'smitten'?" Andrea said with a grin.

"Which one?" Mrs. Pruitt crowed.

"Take your pick," an older lady across the group said.

Kate blushed fiercely. She knew what they were thinking...that Rick and Kate and Joey seemed like a family. She felt as if they were reading her mind.

But they were wrong. All of them.

Alice came to her rescue with a question to the woman sitting across the circle about the built-ins she needed for an organized closet.

Kate was grateful for the time to recover even though it made her realize that Rick's wonderful mother only added to the sense of family.

Every day it became harder for Kate to convince herself that her senses were playing tricks on her. Every day it became harder to even try.

* * *

"All right, Kate," Dr. Lowry said as he placed what was left of Kate's leg cast on the counter behind him. "Let's see if you can put any weight on it."

Rick had to make himself stand still as Kate slid gingerly off the examining table, landing on the only foot that had been supporting her for weeks.

"Better hold on to something at first," the doctor warned.

Given this permission, Rick stepped forward and gave Kate his arm. She grasped it without thinking, adding to the gratification that had been building over the past few weeks as Kate had slowly accepted his help in all kinds of ways.

She took a deep breath and placed her left foot on the floor, unconsciously holding on tighter. She leaned onto her foot, sucking in a pained breath. "It hurts."

"A little or a lot?" the doctor asked.

She bravely leaned on it again. Rick wished he could pick her up and tell her she never had to walk on it again, to spare her another second of pain.

"It's bearable," she admitted.

The doctor nodded. "I doubt much of your pain comes from the bone. You're stretching tendons and muscles you haven't used in over six weeks. They'll have to get used to moving again."

"I'll be fine."

Fine. She always said she was fine, even when he knew good and well that she wasn't.

"Take an over-the-counter pain reliever for any discomfort. Don't go on any 10K runs, but do exercise your leg. It'll probably take a week or so to have your full strength back."

Kate's smile beamed up at Rick. "Just a week."

He tried to smile back, but he couldn't. *Just a week* echoed in his mind. He had *just a week* until Kate would leave, or at least prepare to leave. *Just a week* until Joey's laughter and questions no longer rang through his house, leaving it the empty shell it had been before. *Just a week* until he was lonely once again.

"What's wrong?" Kate watched him closely. "You'll have your house to yourself again. Just think—peace and quiet."

Peace and quiet. In *just a week*. "Can't wait."

His sarcastic tone made her peer at him closely.

To hide his reaction, he turned to open the door for the exiting doctor. *Peace and quiet* was just another way to say *lonely*.

"You sure you're up to this?"

Kate shook her head at Rick's question.

"No?" He smiled with satisfaction. "Good. It's too chilly outside for a walk, anyway."

"It was seventy-three degrees today."

"Maybe. But it's dropped since the sun went down."

"That's beside the point." She stood and placed her hands on her hips. "I was shaking my head because every time during the past three days that I've suggested going for a walk or doing something to build my strength, you try to talk me out of it."

"That's not true."

"You haven't even moved my bed back upstairs."

He stood and faced her. "I'd rather you didn't go up and down them all day while I'm gone. What if your so-called strength gives out and you fall?"

"Mommy goes up the stairs all the time," Joey said as he closed the book he'd been reading.

"What?" Rick's chocolate brown eyes narrowed. "Why?"

"Why not?"

He glowered at her. "Why?"

"That's where the dirty clothes and the plain old dirt is, that's why."

"How many times do I have to tell you that you don't have to clean or cook or anything?"

"You've told me about a million times, which is quite enough."

"Then why do you keep—"

"Listen, you stubborn man." She glowered right back at him. "You're always on my case about letting you do things for me. Yet every time I do something for you, you throw a hissy fit."

He was clearly appalled. "I have never in my life thrown a *hissy* fit."

Her pique vanished at the image, and she smiled. "Well, the male equivalent, then."

He stepped closer. "Kate…"

"Oh, go stuff a potato. If I want to do something for you, I darn well will do it."

"I know," he said with clear disgust. "To repay me."

"No. To make your life a little easier. To give you more time to play Chinese checkers with Joey. To—perhaps one day—see you smile because you know I'm doing whatever I'm doing for you, not to repay you."

Her words took the wind out of his sails.

"Can we play Chinese checkers tonight, Rick?" Joey asked right on cue.

"Sure, Joey." Rick searched Kate's eyes. "After we go for a walk."

"So we're going?" she asked.

"In a minute." He ran a finger along her jaw. "Did you mean it?"

She barely controlled the shiver that ran down her spine at his touch. "That I want to go for a walk?"

He smiled and shook his head. "That what you're doing, you're doing for me, not to repay me."

"Does it matter?"

"Enormously."

She sighed. "It's just that…well, ever since you made such a big deal about it, I've noticed how both you and Joey like having things done for you. And I…well, I kind of like it, too."

He stepped closer and placed his hands on her shoulders. "That's how a real relationship works, you know. You do things for each other just because you want to. Like you said, to make each other's lives a little easier, to give each other more time, to make each other smile."

She was mesmerized by the intensity in his eyes. "That's what I've always heard."

He frowned. "You've never had anyone who did something for you just for the hell of it?"

"Just Joey." She took a deep breath, and her gaze dropped to his lips. "And you."

He placed a finger under her chin and gently forced her to look at him. "I enjoy doing things for you."

Swallowing was hard—from more than the position of her throat. "I know."

He ran a finger across her bottom lip. "I want you to know that if you ever need anything—anything at all—all you have to do is ask me."

"I know." Her voice was whisper soft.

He smiled an even more self-satisfied smile, and his head begin to lower.

Kate waited for the touch of his lips, her breath held, her pulse rising.

"Are you gonna kiss Mommy, Rick?"

The animated question checked all movement.

Then Rick chuckled and without lifting his head, asked, "Should I?"

Kate's breath caught on a sigh.

"If you wanna. Miz Alice asks all the time if you kiss her."

Rick gave Kate a wry smile, squeezed the back of her neck which he'd cupped, then straightened and faced Joey. "Miss Alice asks you that, does she?"

Kate straightened her knit top and placed her cool hands against her burning cheeks. Maybe if she kept repeating to herself that she didn't feel disappointed, she wouldn't.

"Mmm-hmm," Joey said. "Jus' about ever' day."

"And what do you tell her?"

The boy shrugged all the way to his ears. "That I ain't never seen you kiss her."

"*Haven't ever* seen him kiss her...me." Kate frowned, but corrections were easier than explanations.

"Haven't ever," Joey said with exaggeration. "We gonna go for a walk?"

Rick turned to Kate. "You still feel up to it?"

"Yes, of course."

"I'll get your jacket. It's turned chilly since the sun went down."

"All right." Kate smiled. "Thank you."

Rick answered with a grin. "I'll be right back."

"Don't get too far ahead," Rick called to Joey, who was running off extra energy. "Stay where you can see us."

"Yes, sir!" Joey called back.

"That means stop at the corner and wait for us," Kate called.

"Yes, ma'am!"

Rick smiled down at Kate. "Do you believe he will?"

She shrugged. "I believe that if he doesn't, he'll be going to bed as soon as we get home."

Kate blushed as she realized she'd used the word *home*. Hurrying to distract him, she said, "Aren't the stars lovely tonight?"

"Mmm-hmm." Rick's smile turned warmer, and he slipped his hand against hers. He twined their fingers together and walked on. "Clear, cool nights are best for seeing the few you can see through the city lights."

Kate murmured something agreeable.

His hand swallowed hers. His fingers were longer, his palm rougher. The warmth seeped into every corner of her body, sealing the connection that was so much more than physical. The connection that made being with Rick seem like she was finally home.

She loved him.

As soon as the thought formed in her mind, she knew it was true.

It was so sudden and startling, she missed a step.

Rick released her hand to catch her around the waist. "What's wrong? Is your leg hurting?"

She gazed up at him, his warmth now surrounding her entire body. "No, it's fine. Nothing's wrong. Nothing at all."

And she knew that, too, was true as they continued walking.

She should be running away, fearful that this relationship would turn out like the one she had with Mitch. That's what she'd done with every other man who wanted to date her.

But Rick hadn't given her a choice. Circumstances had forced her into his tender care, and somewhere along the way she'd fallen in love with him.

How could she have avoided it? Her fate had been sealed from the beginning, with all the connections she'd felt between them building until they forged a bond that was unbreakable.

She hadn't felt anything like this with Mitch. He'd merely been a side trip, a dead-end on the road to finding the one she was meant to find. How much more obvious could fate be than having her crash into him?

Rick was nothing at all like Mitch. He was a family man from the genes out—responsible, caring, unselfish. A man who wanted a wife who didn't work outside the home, whose work was taking care of the children…and him.

Could she do it? Could she give up her independence so completely? She loved him, but did she love him enough to trust her entire future to him?

And what about Rick?

We're not compatible.

He'd said those words to her only two weeks ago.

But he'd also told her he'd give her whatever she needed.

She needed him. But she also needed to be sure of her own place in the world. Would he give her both? Did he love her, too? Enough? Surely a connection this strong could not be one way.

Just a few minutes ago he'd laid out the requirements in a "real relationship." The question was—did he want a "real" relationship with her?

A few weeks ago she would've said no. She'd been convinced he was only trying to expiate his guilt over Stacy. But he'd told her that though things had started out that way, Stacy hadn't crossed his mind in weeks.

So why hadn't he said anything…if he loved her…if he wanted them to stay? Did he still think she was the kind of person who didn't want him to help her in any way?

She wasn't. Surely he knew.

She could always tell him, she supposed, but that didn't prove anything. Showing him she'd changed was so much better than telling him, and there was one way to clearly show him that she'd become a person who could take as well as give. She would ask his help for something important. Something like…

Finding a job.

Yes, that was perfect.

She would know by his answer how he felt. If he happily offered to help her find employment, she would know that all this time he'd merely been helping someone in need.

But she believed…she hoped…that he would offer her his heart instead.

Chapter Eleven

Rick came downstairs the next morning to find Kate and Joey at the breakfast table. Just as he did every morning, he paused in the doorway to enjoy the sight.

Joey perched backward on the window seat, balancing a glass of milk and watching the birds at the suspended feeder in the condo's tiny backyard. Kate concentrated on the newspaper.

The enticing smells of coffee and some wonderfully baked something filled the air. A plate of homemade muffins on the stove told him what.

He must've died and gone to Heaven in the car crash, just hadn't recognized it. That's the only explanation for the perfect turn his life had taken since then.

Kate must've caught the movement of his head because she looked up and smiled. "Good morning."

Joey half turned with a bright smile. "Hi, Rick!"

"Morning, you two." He walked to the stove and grabbed a muffin. "How long have you been up? Mmm. Geez, these are great. Banana nut's my favorite."

"Me, too," Joey announced.

Kate just smiled. "I know."

Their gazes held for a long moment. If this was what it was like being a ghost, he'd volunteer for the ghost shift the next two or three millennia.

"Can I have a muffin now, too, Mommy?" Joey asked.

She pulled her gaze away. "Yes, baby, of course you can."

She started to rise, but Rick stopped her. "I'll get it."

"Thank you," she said. "The coffee's ready, too."

"I know. I smelled it the moment I woke." He reached into the cabinet for a couple of small plates. "I've been dreaming about it all through my shower."

She chuckled. "Doesn't take much to make you happy, does it?"

She meant it as a joke, but he was dead serious when he said, "No, it doesn't. I'm a simple man with simple needs."

All I need is you, he wanted to say, but he didn't want to scare her.

The thought must've been in his eyes, however, because after a moment she blushed and looked away. "That's good."

Rick placed a muffin on each plate, then he handed one to Joey. The boy carried it carefully to the table while Rick took down two mugs and poured coffee. He doctored his with cream and put both cream and sugar in the other one. Then he took the plate and both coffees to the table.

When he set a mug and muffin in front of Kate, she glanced up in surprise. "Thank you."

"You're welcome." He went back for his own coffee and grabbed another muffin, placing it on a plate so he wouldn't appear to be *too* simple a man. He'd been watching his manners since Joey had been around. Kids learned bad habits early.

When he sat down at the table, he thumbed through the newspaper sections but couldn't find the sports. Only then did he notice what Kate had been concentrating on so hard.

"You're looking at the classifieds." A stupidly obvious observation, but at the moment he didn't feel very clever. At the moment he wanted to grab the section from her hands, rip the entire newspaper to shreds, then cancel his subscription.

"Yes. I'm looking for a job."

At least it wasn't for an apartment. But then, she would need a job before anyone would rent to her.

"But—" Rick wanted to argue, but knew he had no right.

"But what?" She glanced up, then back down. "Oh. The sports is at the front of this section, isn't it?" She began to fold the section up. "Here. I can always look at it later. Unless…"

Hope made his heart return to its normal pattern of beating. "Unless?"

"Perhaps you know of something? I know you have lots of business contacts through Data Enterprises. Do you know if any of them needs a bookkeeper? I could be a secretary, too, I suppose. I'm a very good typist."

Rick was appalled. She was asking him to help her find a job? Why didn't she just ask him to invite ghosts into his house? He'd finally exorcised Stacy's ghost after three long, lonely years. But when Kate and Joey left, they would leave part of their spirits behind…to haunt him.

Rick knew they had to leave sometime. He and Kate wanted different things out of a relationship. He'd known this from practically the moment she woke from the coma.

So, if he knew it, why couldn't he get it through his head? Why did he want her to stay?

Because it was too soon. Kate wasn't strong enough.

He wasn't strong enough.

"No." The word sounded so choked, he took a huge gulp of too-hot coffee. It burned all down his throat. "I don't know anyone who needs…you."

Except me.

Her eyes widened. "Oh. Well. You didn't have to put it that way, did you?"

He realized the insult. "I'm sorry, I—"

"If you don't want to help me, just say so."

She was surprised by his reaction, and she should be. He'd told her just last night that if she needed anything at all, all she had to do was ask.

And here she was asking him for something, something important. He knew it was hard for her just to ask. He should be proud. He should be dancing with joy that she'd asked him.

But he felt as if the room was suddenly short of oxygen.

"I—" he shoved the chair back and stood "—I have to go."

"Rick…"

"Mom wanted me to stop by on the way to work. We'll talk about it later."

"Bye, Rick!"

Joey's call stopped Rick in the doorway. He turned to see the boy's beaming face.

Rick's heart turned over. He loved this boy so much.

Rick's gaze slid to Kate, who watched him with an enigmatic expression. He loved this woman even more.

He knew exactly why he didn't want to let them go. Because being with them felt right. They were family. His family.

No, they weren't. He had to stop thinking that way. Kate obviously didn't return his feelings. She still wanted a "career."

He suddenly realized it wasn't a career he objected to. It was what her insistence on a career meant. It meant she couldn't love him without an insurance policy. It meant she didn't trust him to be there for her, to care for her and Joey.

The pain stabbed so deep he couldn't breathe at all for an endless moment. When he could, he wanted to run away, to find the hole he'd drifted in for three years. There'd been no pain in the hole. Only…deep, dark loneliness.

How could he possibly bring himself to help her? How could she possibly ask it of him?

Then again…how could he not? He loved her, didn't he? Then how could he deny her request? How selfish could he be? When he'd told her he would help her with anything she needed, he hadn't qualified it with "as long as it's what I want, too."

He did love her, and that meant giving her what she needed…even if what she needed wasn't him.

Suddenly an idea came to him, and a light opened at the end of the tunnel. There was a way he could fill Kate's request—quickly—yet keep her in his life on a daily basis.

Maybe all she needed was time. It seemed as if he'd known her forever, but it had only been a few weeks.

And perhaps Kate didn't feel the connection as strongly as he did…yet. Though it seemed as if they were already a family, he and Kate hadn't even been on a proper date. He hadn't spent time courting her, making her love him.

Maybe that's one thing he needed to give her right now—time to be on her own, time to miss him.

Hope made his spirit lift. He returned to the table and sat.

Kate's brow lifted. "I thought Alice needed you."

"This is more important." He met her gaze squarely. "*You're* more important."

She smiled, giving him courage. "Thank you."

"You're welcome. All right. Let's talk. You want a job. I've got one to offer you."

"What?" Her smile faded. "What do you mean?"

"My secretary has been complaining for months about having to work overtime. She does all the office work, payroll, accounts, everything. She could use your help, especially your expertise with the financial part of it."

Kate blinked. "You're offering me a job…at Data Enterprises?"

"That's right. It pays a dollar more an hour than you were going to make at that other job. We have full benefits, even though we're a small company. That's so I can retain the best people. There are ten paid holidays a year, eight fixed and two floating. A week of sick leave and two weeks vacation after a year."

Her gaze had dropped to the table halfway through his recitation. "I see. It sounds…nice."

"I think you'll enjoy working there." He studied what he could see of her face. "What do you think?"

Her eyes lifted to his then. They were filled with hurt. She looked as if he'd just broken her heart.

What had he done, except given her what she wanted?

"I think I'm not quite as pathetic as you seem to think I am."

He sat bolt-upright in his chair. "Pathetic? I didn't say you were—"

"You don't have to create a job for me, Mr. McNeal. I can get one—a real one—on my own. I'm a good worker. My ex-boss will testify to that. He hated to lose me."

"I'm sure that's true. But this *is* a real job. Judy's been on my case for months. With the accident and everything, I haven't had time to—"

"Right. You just happen to mention it now. How convenient."

He drove his hands through his hair. "What's wrong? You asked me if I knew of anyone who needed you. Well, I need you."

"Yeah, Mommy. Rick needs you."

Joey had been so quiet, Rick had all but forgotten he was there.

Evidently, so had Kate. "Joey, please go upstairs and make your bed."

"I can do it later, Mommy. I wanna stay here."

"Joey, please. Do it now."

The boy looked at Rick. "Do I gotta?"

"Joey!" Kate's voice was both hurt and questioning.

Rick was touched that Joey had turned to him…like any son would seek justice from his dad when he didn't like his mother's ruling. It was good to know he'd won over one of the Burnetts. If only he could reach the one who made the decisions. "Always obey your mother, Joey."

"Awwww. Yes, sir." Joey slowly, reluctantly climbed down from the window seat and trudged out the kitchen door.

"Thank you," Kate said when they heard him on the stairs.

"For backing you up? It's what people in relationships do. I'm not out to steal your son from you. All I want to do is make you see reason."

"Reason," she said sarcastically. "What reason is there for me to accept a job you've created just for me? It isn't good for my self-esteem, and it makes you look bad in front of your employees, which can't be good for Data Enterprises."

He tried to hide his growing frustration. Why didn't she understand? "I have to create the job, anyway. Data Enterprises has grown phenomenally as computers are used more and more. I need to hire a couple more programmers, too. I'll need you even more then...to back me up. Payroll is a sensitive area. I need someone I can trust."

She searched his face, as if trying to find the truth there. He didn't flinch, because he was telling the truth.

"You'd be helping me tremendously, because I won't have to waste time and money searching for a good employee. I know you, and I know you'll do a good job." Rick stressed his words with strong gestures. "From your standpoint, you'd save a lot of time. Finding a good job can take weeks. Sometimes months."

Again she said nothing, just studied his face. Hers held no expression. He couldn't tell what she was thinking. Where was the connection when he needed it most?

"Think about it. There's no need to decide anything today." He paused, but when she remained silent, he pushed, "All right?"

Her gaze dropped to the table. "All right."

He sat back with a sigh. He hadn't realized how tense he'd become. "I think I'll stay home today. There's some paperwork I brought home—"

"No!" She almost shouted the word, then visibly calmed herself. "How can I think about anything with you hovering all day? Go to work. Please."

He took a moment to search her face, but he still couldn't read positive or negative. "All right. But I'll be home early, around three."

She nodded, but didn't watch him as he left the room.

Kate didn't need to think about his offer.

Even if his job offer was real, she couldn't work for him. If the relationship that seemed to be budding turned sour— if he left like all men did eventually—then she'd be back in the same position she was in now.

She needed a job that provided real support. Support she could count on by becoming a valuable employee through hard work. Support she—

Kate stopped in midthought.

She didn't trust him. That's what all her logical arguments were saying. She didn't trust him to stay. Didn't trust his love. Didn't even trust that he did love her.

If she had a good, steady job, *she* was the one in control. She didn't have to trust him. The job was her escape hatch. Her ace in the hole.

What did this mean? Did it mean she didn't love him?

She obviously didn't love him enough to give him what he wanted—which was a wife who didn't work. She didn't love him enough to trust him.

Maybe she could never love anyone, except Joey. Maybe her childhood had scarred her too deeply and she was too flawed to love anyone...or for anyone to love.

The grief that welled up inside at that possibility nearly made her faint. To relieve the pressure, she bent her mind to logical, practical matters.

Like where all of this left her and Rick.

She didn't love him enough to give him what he wanted, and he didn't love her enough to give her what she wanted.

Tears sprang to Kate's eyes, but she forced them back. Crying wasn't going to do her any good, and she'd just have to explain her red eyes to Joey.

She needed to concentrate on what *would* do her good. She needed to *do* something. Something positive. Something that would make her feel that she was once again in control of her life.

The only way to do that was to leave.

The tears threatened to return—along with sheer panic—at the thought. She squeezed her eyes tight so she wouldn't give in to either.

She couldn't stay.

Rick might want her, but wanting was not loving. She and Joey had been flesh-and-blood stand-ins for Rick's dead wife and son. That's all.

The realization cut deep, but there was nothing she could do about it. She couldn't make Rick love her.

Rick still wasn't over his wife—probably never would be. The hole he'd dug for himself after Stacy died three years ago was too deep and steep for him to ever climb out.

Kate swallowed with difficulty.

Yet, how could she leave, from a purely practical standpoint? She had no money, no friends, no resources of any kind. And even if she did, how could she ask anyone to—

Her eyes popped open.

No. She had to stop thinking like that. She did have friends in Memphis. She had Alice and Andrea and several other ladies from the church.

Ask and you shall receive.

That's what the preacher said last Sunday. Only one way to find out if it was true. She would call Alice to see if she knew of anyone who had a room to spare for a few weeks.

With new purpose, she rose and picked up the kitchen phone. Then she hesitated. Alice was Rick's mother, who seemed hell-bent on marrying Kate off to her son. Would a matchmaking mother help the potential bride move out?

Kate believed so. Alice didn't seem like the kind of person to beat a dead horse. Kate briefly thought about calling Andrea instead, but she knew Alice much better.

Taking a calming breath, Kate dialed her number.

Alice picked up after two rings. "Hello?"

"Alice? This is Kate."

"Hello, dear. What's going on today? You need me to pick up Joey?"

"No. Well, yes, in a manner of speaking."

"What manner?"

Kate leaned a hip against the counter. "We're moving out."

"What? You and Joey? Today?"

"Yes."

"But, Kate, you—"

"I know you wanted me to marry your son, Alice, but Rick still loves Stacy. I think he always will."

"Well, of course he always will. She was a huge part of his life for fifteen years. That doesn't mean he can't love you, too."

"He doesn't."

"How do you know? Did he tell you?"

"He showed me, in a way that couldn't be clearer. He offered me a job."

"A job? At Data Enterprises? And this is bad because…?"

"Because he doesn't trust me enough to offer me his heart." Kate squeezed the phone tighter. "But it's me, too. Neither one of us is ready for this kind of commitment. I need to leave, Alice. I have to be out on my own."

Alice sighed. "I'll be over in an hour."

"Do you know anyone Joey and I can stay with for a couple of weeks? Just until I find a job and an apartment?"

"You'll stay with me." She sounded offended that Kate would suggest otherwise.

"But your construction—"

"Is at a standstill."

"It is? Why?"

"I special ordered bathroom fixtures, and the supplier sent the wrong ones. The contractor took a short-term job while we're waiting on them."

"Are you sure you have room for us?"

"As long as you don't mind the mess, we'll make do."

"Thank you, Alice. I'll go pack." Kate heaved a sigh of relief. "It won't take long."

Rick knew something wasn't right the instant he walked in the door. He'd ended up staying the full day at work, but there were no smells of supper cooking, no Kate humming in the kitchen, no Joey running to greet him.

"Kate?" He placed his briefcase on the chest in the hall. "Joey?"

Silence answered him.

Rick strode down the hall to the kitchen. Nothing. No one.

"Where are you?" he called as he raced up the stairs, only a little faster than his heart.

Joey's neat room didn't alarm him. Kate always made him keep it clean.

Had they gone somewhere with his mother?

They'd always told him when they weren't going to be home.

He headed downstairs, intending to call his mother. Detouring through the dining room, he stopped short. Kate's bed had been stripped. Completely.

Rick's heart stopped, too.

Neither the blanket nor the sheets were anywhere around.

Spinning on his heel, he flung open the hall closet where she'd kept her clothes. The only garments hanging there were the coat and jackets he'd shoved to one side. The blanket was folded neatly on the shelf above.

They were gone?

Unable to accept his conclusion, he ran back upstairs to Joey's room. The drawers in the chest were empty. So was the closet.

The guest bathroom was devoid of tooth and hair brushes. The only thing that lingered was the scent of Kate's hand lotion.

In utter disbelief, Rick leaned heavily against the cool tile.

Gone. They were gone. Without telling him. Without saying goodbye. Without even a thank-you or a kiss-my—

Why? All he'd done was offer Kate a job. Isn't that what she wanted? She'd asked him to help her find one.

She'd asked him.

He'd taught her something, at least.

But at the moment, the realization didn't make him happy. He hadn't taught her to need him, hadn't taught her to love him.

Grief greater than he'd ever known welled up inside him, filling his chest, threatening to cut off his air supply.

She didn't need him.

Nothing could wound him more.

Wheeling about, Rick stumbled into the hall. How could he hurt this much, yet be so numb he could barely feel his feet?

He briefly thought about calling his mother to ask if she knew where Kate had gone, but dismissed the idea. He was too raw. He didn't want anyone to know—not just yet— that Kate had left him. In a different way than Stacy, perhaps, but just as completely.

He stood at the top of the stairs and felt the emptiness of the house close in around him. A lone wolf... wounded...ready to howl at the moon.

Chapter Twelve

"**Y**ou're here rather late."

It took several seconds for Rick to pull his attention from the engrossing problem of nested subforms that weren't performing properly. When his mind came back to reality, he looked up from his office computer to see Chester Bradon, his second in command, leaning against the doorway.

Rick glanced at the menu bar on his screen. "It's only 9:40. I've been here much later than this on many occasions."

"Not in the past six weeks," Chester said.

A muscle in Rick's jaw twitched. "Your point?"

"Just thought you had better things to do these days."

"You're still here. Don't *you* have anything better to do?"

Chester shrugged. "I'm just killing time until the bars start hopping."

"On a Thursday night? Tomorrow's a workday, you know."

"That's why I'm going at ten rather than twelve. Have

to time it for the ultimate chickfest. On a weeknight ten is optimum."

Rick turned back to his computer. "Have fun."

"Why don't you come with me?"

"I have work to do."

"You're working on that nested subform for Delta Supply, aren't you?"

Rick didn't reply. He'd been desperate for something to keep busy, and he knew Chester knew it.

"How is Charlene ever going to learn to find the bugs in her work if you do it for her?"

"I'll show her what I did."

"It's not the same."

Rick glowered at Chester over his shoulder. "Who's the boss around here?"

"I'm the one who kept up with the workflow since your accident."

Rick let go of his pique reluctantly. "And you did a damn good job."

"Come on. Let's go to The Fox's Lair. It will do you good. You can't stay buried forever."

"Why not?"

"Rick…"

"Hell." The anger he'd been existing on for two days flooded back. Anger at Kate, anger at the world, anger at himself. Rick shoved a disk into his zip drive and backed up the file he'd been working on. "If it will make you happy, I'll quit for tonight. But I have zero interest in a 'chickfest.'"

As he waited for the file to copy, Rick could feel Chester watching him from the doorway. "What?"

"What happened to Kate?"

"Who?"

"Yeah, right."

Rick cursed under his breath. Employees shouldn't know their boss so well. Too much familiarity encouraged insubordination. "Kate is gone."

It was Chester's turn to curse. "I was kinda hoping…"

"What?" Rick demanded harshly.

"That you and she…" He sighed. "You seemed to really care about her. I don't remember you acting so loopy before, even over Stacy. Even when you and Stacy got married."

Rick retrieved the disk his zip drive spit out, then put his computer to sleep. "Yeah, well, life goes on."

"*I* know that. The question is…do you?"

Rick stood and leaned stiff arms on the desk in his best alpha-male posture. "Who the hell are you to—"

"Okay. All right." Chester held his hands up defensively. "I know when I'm not wanted. Work all night. I don't care. See you in the morning."

Rick stayed where he was until he heard the dead bolt click on the front door. Then he dropped his head and stared at the desk.

He briefly considered waking up his computer and continuing Charlene's work. But Chester was right. People learned more from mistakes than successes.

That meant the only place he had to go was home.

Damn.

He'd stayed late at work tonight and the past two nights because too many ghosts roamed his condo. The empty rooms echoed with—

Rick straightened suddenly and muttered, "Get over it, McNeal. Kate is gone, and there's not a damn thing you can do about it."

He grabbed his briefcase, slung the light jacket he'd worn that morning over his shoulder and headed out the door.

The condo was his home, for God's sake. A place with rooms and furniture, where he ate and slept. The only ghosts were in his mind.

So he was alone? Lots of people were alone. Many of them chose to live their lives that way.

And if he didn't want to be alone, he needed to get out

and circulate. He *could* fall in love again. Kate at least had taught him that. Stacy was not the only love of his life.

So Kate didn't want him. Fine.

He fell in love with her. He could fall in love again.

Driven in a new direction, Rick locked the door to Data Enterprises and headed for his new Jeep.

The Fox's Lair sounded like a good place to meet women.

By the time he reached his Jeep, however, he knew he wasn't going there. Not only were bars not his style, but as he'd thought about the women he would meet, he realized he just wasn't interested.

Not one of them would be Kate. Not one of them could even compare.

He wasn't just lonely. He was lonely for one particular woman—Kate.

He leaned on the door of his Jeep and closed his eyes to shut out the picture of her lifting her face for him to kiss the night before she left. Instead of going away, the picture sharpened.

He wished now that he'd kissed her, even in front of Joey. He wished that he'd told her that he loved her and wanted her to stay with him forever.

Why hadn't he? It wasn't like him to be a coward. It wasn't like him not to go after what he wanted. That's how he'd started Data Enterprises. That's how he'd won Stacy's heart in the ninth grade. That's how—

No. That wasn't right.

He'd been that way before Stacy died, but in the last few years he *had* been a coward. Instead of going after the things he wanted—like Kate—he'd turned his back on life, turned his heart away from who he was.

That was about to change.

Kate wanted a career. All right, he could live with—

Suddenly all the things Kate had been saying to him about her childhood, about Joey's father and about having a career jelled in his mind. It wasn't a career she wanted, necessarily. She wanted control over her life.

When she was a child, she certainly didn't have control. She was either at the mercy of a mother who was spineless and lazy, or shoved into this home or that by the state.

The only time she'd ever had control was when she'd been on her own, working to support herself and Joey.

Then Rick crashed into her life and wrested control away from her again. He insisted on doing everything for her, from carrying her around to making all the decisions about the insurance settlement.

And to top it off, he'd offered her a job—another form of control.

Damn. How could he have been so stupid? No wonder she left.

How could he ever make it up to her? Would she even let him try?

She had to. She was his woman. His mate. For life.

Surely she knew that he was hers.

He'd make her understand. Understand that *he* understood. He knew what she needed, and he was more than willing to give it to her. In fact, he was determined to give it to her.

If she'd come back into his life, she could do anything she wanted. Go back to work, stay at home, go back to school for her degree so she could have a real career. They could hire a nanny to take care of their kids.

The decision made, Rick climbed into his Jeep and glanced at his watch. After ten.

Damn. He wouldn't be able to find Kate tonight. Since he had no idea where else to start, the first call had to be to his mother and she—

Uh-oh. He hadn't called his mother in two days. She was going to be hopping mad. And since she went to bed at nine-thirty, he didn't want to call and make her even angrier.

He'd have to wait until morning.

Damn.

* * *

Kate paused just outside the door to Alice's living room as she overheard Joey ask the question he'd asked a hundred times in the last two days.

"Did Rick call yet?"

Alice answered Joey patiently, bless her. It had been all Kate could do not to tell Joey he shouldn't hold his breath because Rick wasn't going to call, because he didn't want them. At least, he didn't want her.

Dragging her mind away from the knife that stabbed her heart, Kate focused on Alice and Joey's conversation.

"Do you know what an ostrich is?" Alice asked.

"You mean the big bird with the long legs and long neck?"

"Yes, that's right. You're so smart, little one."

Kate could picture Alice mussing Joey's hair like she always did.

"I know," Joey said matter-of-factly.

Alice chuckled. "It's a good thing to know. Always remember that you're smart, especially when you're dealing with stupid people. Like Rick."

The last phrase was muttered, but Kate could hear.

So could Joey. "Huh? Rick's stupid?"

"Remember the ostrich we were talking about?"

"Uh-huh."

"Well, Rick's being an ostrich. Know what an ostrich does?"

"Umm. Oh, yeah. It puts its head in a hole...or something."

"That's right. When an ostrich doesn't want to deal with something, it buries its head in the sand."

"Rick's head is in the sand?" Joey sounded confused. "Is that why he didn't call?"

Kate smiled at Joey's literal conclusion.

"Yep," Alice said with smug self-satisfaction.

"Why don't you tell him to get it out?"

"Because he hasn't called in two days. And if he did, I'd tell him just where to put his—"

"How do I look?" Kate cut off Alice's comment by stepping into the room. She executed a runway turn to let them see the light-blue silk suit Alice had bought Kate for job interviews. "Would you hire me?"

"You look gooooood, Mommy."

"Oh, my yes," Alice exclaimed. "You do look good in that suit. Do I have excellent taste or what?"

Kate leaned over and kissed her cheek. "Yes, you do. Thank you."

Alice waved her away. "Just go knock 'em dead."

"You're sure it's okay if I take your car?"

"How else are you going to get there?"

"I could take a cab."

Alice shook her head vigorously. "I'm not doing a single thing this morning except playing with my little man here. You go on and do whatever you need to do. We'll be just fine."

Kate met Alice's gaze. "Am I doing the right thing?"

Alice smiled kindly. "Only you can answer that, dear."

Kate took a deep breath. "I know. I am. Thank you, Alice." Kate spread her arms toward Joey. "Can I have a good-luck kiss?"

He ran to hug her. "Good luck, Mommy. Knock 'em dead!"

Kate chuckled and mussed his hair herself. "I'll sure try, baby."

"H'lo?"

"Joey?" Rick's heart soared. Kate had gone to his mother's. A good sign. Why would she go there if she didn't want any contact with him? She knew he saw his mother on a daily basis. Well…usually. "How are you, little guy?"

"Rick?" Joey's voice escalated. "That you?"

"It's me. Sorry I haven't been around to tuck you in bed."

"I know. You been in the sand."

Rick hesitated. "Sand? I have?"

"Uh-huh. Miz Alice said you was an ostrich with your head in the sand." Joey made it sound like such a sad prospect. And it was.

"Miss Alice is right. But I'm never going to be an ostrich again, okay? Too much sand gets in my eyes."

"Did it make you sleepy? Is that why you didn't call?"

"Sleepy? Oh. As in the Sand Man." Rick chuckled. Joey was so good at making connections. "I've really missed you, little guy. Your mom, too."

"I miss you, too. So does Mom."

"Is your mother there?"

"Nope."

Rick frowned. "Is Miss Alice taking care of you?"

"Yep. You coming over, Rick?"

"In a little while, but for now I need to find your mother. Can you call Miss Alice to the phone?"

"Miz Alice! Miz Alice! Rick called!"

Rick had to hold the phone away from his ear, but he grinned at his son's enthusiasm. His son. He liked the sound of those words. And with Joey, they felt right.

"Oh, he finally did, did he?"

"Uh-huh."

"Hel—"

"Where's Kate?" Rick asked before his mother could finish.

There was a noticeable pause. "Who is this?"

Taken aback, Rick hesitated. "What do you mean, who is this? This is your son. You knew before you came to the phone. Joey told you."

"Son?" She sniffed. "Hmm. Now that you mention it, I do seem to recall a painful time in the hospital thirty-three years ago."

"All right, Mom. I get it. Sorry I haven't called."

"It's been two days."

"I know. I'm sorry. Believe me, you don't know how sorry I am."

"I thought about calling the police."

"No, you didn't. You know what happened. You know Kate moved out, because obviously she and Joey moved in with you."

"You're darned tootin' I know she moved out. I helped her."

"You helped…" He toned down his voice, but only because he was speaking to his mother. When he thought about the suffering he'd been through in the past two days, he had to ask, "How could you do that to your only child?"

"Because my only child offered the woman he loves a job instead of a ring…which should come with unconditional love and support. I thought I taught you more about the power of love than that. About trusting the ones you love." Alice sniffed again. "Besides, who would Kate turn to but her future mother-in-law? I *am* going to be her mother-in-law, aren't I?"

"As soon as I can find her and talk her into having me. But first you have to tell me where she is."

"She's on a job interview."

"Already? Where?"

"International Paper."

"Thanks, Mom. I'll let you know."

"You're not going there, are you?"

"Yes, ma'am, I am. I know where the human resources office is. Did she take your car?"

"Yes, but you can't go barging in on her interview."

"Give me some credit. I'm not going in at all. But I am going to camp out on the hood of your car until she comes out."

"Then what?"

"Then I'm going to show her that she's worth fighting for."

* * *

Kate frowned as she walked out the door of International Paper. She was certain she was going to be offered the job, even though there was one more applicant to interview.

So why wasn't she jumping for joy? Why was she depressed?

She stopped at the top of the short flight of steps leading down to the parking lot and leaned against the railing.

This felt wrong. This felt as if she were betraying someone or something.

No, not some*thing*. She had to be honest with herself. And it wasn't just someone. It was Rick.

But that couldn't be right. She'd decided two days ago that she didn't love him enough to give up having a career. The possibility of not having something to support her if he left scared her witless.

But then...not having Rick scared her, too.

Great. Just great. Why was she always getting into these damned-if-she-did-and-damned-if-she-didn't situations?

She slowly descended the steps.

The question was...which scared her least?

Kate shook her head.

No. That way of looking at things was too negative. She should ask herself which would make her happiest—having a career or having Rick?

Stepping onto the sidewalk, she stopped.

The answer was obvious. She'd had a "career" for the past six years and aside from having Joey, those years hadn't made her particularly happy. In fact, those years had only fed her fear.

But these last weeks with Rick...

She smiled. Yes. She'd been very happy living with him, doing things for him, waiting for him to come home at the end of the day and hearing him call her "beautiful Kate."

So what was she doing here? Why wasn't she rushing to his house or—she checked her watch—to Data Enterprises and telling him she loved him?

She hurried toward Alice's car, but slowed after just a few steps.

What about the trust issue? Did she trust him enough to let him have control of her life?

Kate's eyes focused then, and she saw the man sitting on the hood of Alice's car three rows over. She recognized him instantly, and her heart skipped a beat.

Had she conjured Rick by thinking about him? Or was she thinking about him because the connection between them told her he was here?

She felt the connection now. It extended between them like a rope of light—stretched tight, contracting as it inexorably pulled them together.

Uncertain of his motives, she resisted, walking slowly toward him.

Rick slid off the hood of Alice's Buick. He waited there, watching her as she moved closer.

She felt his gaze on her like hands, caressing, stroking.

He was dressed in jeans and a light-blue chambray shirt she'd washed several times. The soft cotton stretched across his broad shoulders and chest. The cool morning breeze pressed it against the ridges and planes of his body. She knew what the fabric felt like in her hands. She knew what those hard muscles felt like beneath them.

The memory—incredibly vivid—stole her breath.

Rick's scrutiny was so tangible, so unreadable, Kate stopped a car width away. "Why are you here?"

"I came to see you," he said. "How did your interview go?"

"Interview..." It took a moment for Kate's mind to switch from the surprise of him being there back to the interview. "It went well. Very well."

His jaw muscles tightened. "Did you take the job?"

"I wasn't offered it."

When he scowled and looked as if he was about to go give International Paper a piece of his mind for passing her over, she qualified her statement. "Yet. They still have one more applicant to interview."

He moved a step closer. "I see."

She forced her eyes away from his handsome face. "Mr. Halsey was very encouraging, though. He likes me a lot."

"Who wouldn't?"

His simple, unexpected reply touched her so deeply that closing her eyes was her only defense against the emotion.

"Kate…"

Suddenly the connection between them sent sparks showering all around, and she opened her eyes to see him barely a foot away.

"I'm sorry," he whispered.

His brown eyes were so intense, so deep, she felt as if she were drowning in a sweet, warm, intoxicating pool of chocolate. "For what?"

"For being a coward. For being ten times a fool. Instead of coming after you and dragging you back into my arms, I crawled back into the hole I've haunted for years. I have no excuse except…it hurt when you and Joey went away, and the hole was comfortable. The hole was home for so many years."

"The hole is lonely, Rick."

"I know. Believe me, I know that very, very well." His strong fingers lifted, hesitated, then gently stroked her jaw. "You came into my life and tore the cover off my hidey hole once. Will you do it again…beautiful Kate?"

Her breath caught, but though her heart was melting, she didn't give in. She couldn't. Not yet. There was still the trust issue to resolve. "Looks as if you've done it yourself."

He shook his head. "Only to come looking for you. If you don't save me from myself, I might go back in and never see daylight again. I need you, Kate. Come live with me and take care of me."

"Take…" So many emotions that she couldn't name them all swirled inside her—twisting, tumbling over themselves, expanding so much she could barely breathe. "Take care of you? I thought you wanted to take care of me."

Without seeming to move, he suddenly was so close she could feel the warmth of his body through the silk of her suit. He cradled her face in his large hands and gazed down at her intently. "Can't we take care of each other? Isn't that what love is?"

"Love?" She tried to swallow, but couldn't. "You love me?"

"With all my heart...and soul...and more passion than I've ever known."

A tear escaped. "Oh, Rick..."

"My love for Stacy grew as we grew up. There was passion, sure, but nothing like I feel for you. It was a quieter, gentler love. It took a long time for me to recognize what I feel for you as love. Even then, I didn't trust it to stick around...one way or another."

"You didn't trust *me* to stick around? I felt the same about—" Kate sucked in a horrified breath. "And then I didn't stick around, did I? I left you. You're the one who was constant. You're the one who wasn't going to leave." Tears burned her eyes. "Oh, Rick, how can you ever forgive me?"

"I can forgive you anything...because I love you." He lifted her chin. "When you left, I went through hell. But it took you leaving for me to see how stupid I am. I haven't been the man I was meant to be. I turned my back on life. I turned my back on myself."

She slipped her arms around his neck. "But I love the man you've been the past six weeks. Please don't tell me you're going to change."

He wrapped his arms around her waist and pulled her tight against him. "You love me?"

"Of course I do. Only someone who loves deeply can be hurt as deeply as I was when you offered me the job at Data Enterprises."

"All I was thinking was that I had to have you in my

life. I thought we hadn't had enough time to fall in love. Or rather, that you hadn't had enough time. I thought I would scare you away if I moved too fast."

"You think too much." Her eyes dropped to his lips. "All I wanted was your trust…and your heart."

He took her hint and covered her mouth with his. The kiss was warm, deep, promising. When he drew away, he whispered, "My heart was already yours. All you have to do—" he kissed her again "—is take it. Will you?"

She smiled against his mouth. "Yes."

"And keep it forever…safe and sound?"

She nibbled on his ear. "And out of hidey holes."

He chuckled and squeezed her tight. "I love you so much."

"I love you, too."

"Let's go home."

"Yes."

As he turned her in his arms to head for their cars, he spied the building she'd just left and stopped. "Will you take this job if they offer it?"

She shook her head. "I'm going to take care of you…and as many children as you want."

His eyes shone with love, but then he shook his head. "Kate, I don't want to control you. I don't want to keep you—how did you put it? Barefoot and pregnant and ignorant. You are free to do anything you want to do. Stay home. Take this job. But…"

"Yes?"

"I have a suggestion." He pulled her around so she faced him, and wrapped his arms around her waist. "If a career is important to you, why not go back to school? You can finish your degree in accounting or whatever you like. We can hire a nanny to take care of the kids. Or maybe Mom wants the job."

She peered at him closely. "You really wouldn't mind if I have a career?"

"As long as you come home to me at night and kiss me goodbye every morning. For the rest of our lives."

She felt so much love for this warm wonderful man, she had to be glowing. She ran a finger down his jaw. "We can discuss nannies and careers and everything else later. But first I have to ask if you'll do something for me."

"I'll do *anything* for you."

Kate's heart turned over. She didn't know until now that she'd been waiting all her life to hear those words. "Will you marry me?"

Laughing, Rick grabbed her around the waist and whirled her around. "I thought you'd never ask!"

Epilogue

A Year Later

Rick leaned back against the stout tree trunk and took a deep breath of the warm, humid air. The summer breeze felt good on his face. It felt like life.

He smiled.

"What's so amusing?" Kate asked softly.

He looked down at her. She lay with her head in his lap—the way she had over a year ago, after the accident. How far they had come since then.

This time she was stretched out on the blanket they'd spread beneath the park tree, gazing up at him. Her eyes glowed with love...for him.

His heart tumbled over itself. "Nothing. Everything. I'm just happy."

"Happy that I'll finally graduate in August?" she teased. "Or about the baby?"

She'd told him the night before that she was pregnant. They'd celebrated all night long.

"Of course I'm happy you're going to graduate, and I'm

ecstatic about having a baby.'' He stroked a short strand of
wavy blond hair from her temple. The scar there was still
noticeable, but grew fainter every day. ''But mostly I'm
happy about us.''

She smiled tenderly and turned her head to kiss his hand.
''Have I told you today that I love you?''

''No, Mrs. McNeal, you haven't.''

''Sorry to have been so neglectful, Mr. McNeal.'' Her
beautiful blue eyes locked with his. ''I love you.''

His smile spread from ear to ear, and his heart filled with
gratitude. ''I know. You show me in so many ways, every
day...and every night.''

She chuckled. ''Well, in case you don't know, that's how
I became pregnant.''

His hand reached down to cover her stomach. ''You've
made me so happy. I cherish each day that I wake up to
see your smile.''

Her hands covered his. ''How many children do you
want?''

''We never did discuss numbers, did we?''

She shook her head.

''How about a hundred? Especially if they're all as special as Joey.''

''A hundred?'' She laughed. ''Somehow that doesn't
sound like fun.''

''Making them would be.''

She smiled. ''You've got me there.''

''How about two more after this one?'' he asked.

''That sounds doable. Another boy and then a girl for
them to terrorize.''

His gaze lifted to Joey, who played happily and noisily
with several other children on the playground. They'd
picked him up from Vacation Bible School at noon, treated
him to a McDonalds lunch where they'd informed him of
his pending brotherhood, then brought him to the local park
to celebrate. ''Somehow I can't picture Joey terrorizing
anyone.''

"Hmm. Probably not. But you never know. You're making inroads every day, undoing my early training."

Rick studied her beautiful face.

"What?" she asked when he didn't say anything.

"Thank you."

"For what? Getting pregnant? I didn't do it on my own, you know."

"Thank you for bringing me back to life."

Her smile softened, and she reached up to caress his jaw. "It was…and continues to be…my pleasure."

"A year ago I thought I could never love anyone the way I loved Stacy. And I was right."

A storm began brewing across Kate's lovely face. "But you said—"

He pressed a finger across her lips. "My love for you goes so far beyond my feelings for Stacy, it's like comparing bytes with gigabytes. She was my first love, but you're the love of my life."

Her crystal-blue eyes filled with tears. "Oh, Rick, my sweet loving husband. You've made me incredibly happy. I need you more every day."

His heart filled with so much love, surely the universe had expanded just to contain it all. "I'll be here for you every day. You can count on that." He bent to touch his lips to hers. "You can count on me."

"I do, my love." She pulled his lips back to hers with the hand she'd wrapped around his neck. "I always will."

* * * * *

CALL THE ONES YOU LOVE OVER THE HOLIDAYS!

Save $25 off future book purchases when you buy any four Harlequin® or Silhouette® books in October, November and December 2001,

PLUS

receive a phone card good for 15 minutes of long-distance calls to anyone you want in North America!

WHAT AN INCREDIBLE DEAL!

Just fill out this form and attach 4 proofs of purchase (cash register receipts) from October, November and December 2001 books, and Harlequin Books will send you a coupon booklet worth a total savings of $25 off future purchases of Harlequin® and Silhouette® books, AND a 15-minute phone card to call the ones you love, anywhere in North America.

Please send this form, along with your cash register receipts as proofs of purchase, to:
In the USA: Harlequin Books, P.O. Box 9057, Buffalo, NY 14269-9057
In Canada: Harlequin Books, P.O. Box 622, Fort Erie, Ontario L2A 5X3
Cash register receipts must be dated no later than December 31, 2001.
Limit of 1 coupon booklet and phone card per household.
Please allow 4-6 weeks for delivery.

I accept your offer! Please send me my coupon booklet and a 15-minute phone card:

Name: _____

Address: _____ City: _____

State/Prov.: _____ Zip/Postal Code: _____

Account Number (if available): _____

---

097 KJB DAGL
PHQ4012

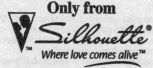

where love comes alive—online...

eHARLEQUIN.com

shop eHarlequin

♥ Find all the new Silhouette releases at everyday great discounts.

♥ Try before you buy! Read an excerpt from the latest Silhouette novels.

♥ Write an online review and share your thoughts with others.

reading room

♥ Read our Internet exclusive daily and weekly online serials, or vote in our interactive novel.

♥ Talk to other readers about your favorite novels in our Reading Groups.

♥ Take our Choose-a-Book quiz to find the series that matches you!

authors' alcove

♥ Find out interesting tidbits and details about your favorite authors' lives, interests and writing habits.

♥ Ever dreamed of being an author? Enter our Writing Round Robin. The Winning Chapter will be published online! Or review our writing guidelines for submitting your novel.

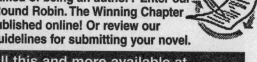

All this and more available at
www.eHarlequin.com
on Women.com Networks

SINTB1R